Christmas Sparkle Collection
Six Stories in One

Join the **Rainbow Magic Reading Challenge!**

Read the story and collect your fairy points to climb the
Reading Rainbow at the back of the book.

This book is worth 4 stars.

Special thanks to
Rachel Elliot &
Narinder Dhami

ORCHARD BOOKS

Holly the Christmas Fairy first published in Great Britain in 2004 by Orchard Books
Stella the Star Fairy Fairy first published in Great Britain in 2005 by Orchard Books
This collection first published in Great Britain in 2021 by The Watts Publishing Group

1 3 5 7 9 10 8 6 4 2

© 2004, 2005 Rainbow Magic Limited
© 2004, 2005 HIT Entertainment Limited
Illustrations © Georgie Ripper 2004
Illustrations © Orchard Books 2005

A CIP catalogue record for this book is available from the British Library.

ISBN 978 1 40836 691 2

Printed and bound in Great Britain

The paper and board used in this book are made from wood from responsible sources

Orchard Books
An imprint of Hachette Children's Group
Part of The Watts Publishing Group Limited
Carmelite House, 50 Victoria Embankment, London EC4Y 0DZ

An Hachette UK Company
www.hachette.co.uk
www.hachettechildrens.co.uk

Christmas Sparkle Collection
Six Stories in One

By Daisy Meadows

ORCHARD

www.orchardseriesbooks.co.uk

Fairyland
Palace

The Park

Kirsty's House

Wetherbury Village

Hillfields Farm

HILLFIELDS
FARM

Christmas
Trees

Tippington
Town

The Fairyland Christmas Tree

Jack Frost's Ice Castle

The Market Square

Goblin Grotto

Santa's Cabin

RAINBOW SHOPPING CENTRE

Rachel's House

Shopping Centre

Holly the Christmas Fairy
Contents

Story One:
Santa's Missing Sleigh

Story Two:
A Narrow Escape

Story Three:
The Night Before Christmas

Stella the Star Fairy
Contents

Story One:
The Magical Missing Candle

Story Two:
Snowballs and Baubles

Story Three:
Search for the Star

Jack Frost's Spell

Christmas plans may go awry,
If I can make these reindeer fly.
Santa's gifts for girls and boys
Shall all become my sweets and toys!

Magic reindeer listen well,
As now I bind you with this spell.
Heed my bidding, fly this sleigh
Through starry skies and far away.

Holly the
Christmas Fairy

Story One
Santa's Missing Sleigh

Chapter One
A Magical Mistake

"Only three days to go!" Rachel
Walker sighed happily. She was pinning
Christmas cards onto long pieces of
red ribbon, ready to hang on the living-
room wall. "I love Christmas! Don't you,
Kirsty?"

Kirsty Tate, Rachel's best friend,

nodded. "Of course I do," she replied, handing Rachel another pile of cards. "It's a magical time, isn't it?"

Rachel and Kirsty laughed, and touched the golden lockets they both wore around their necks. The two girls shared a marvellous, magical secret. No one else knew it but they were friends with the fairies!

Kirsty and Rachel had visited Fairyland several times when their help had been needed. The first time, they had rescued the Rainbow Fairies after they were banished by Jack Frost's nasty spell. Then Jack Frost and his goblin servants had stolen the magic tail feathers from Doodle, the cockerel in charge of fairy weather. The girls had helped the Weather Fairies to get Doodle's feathers back.

In return, the Fairy King and Queen had given gold lockets to Rachel and Kirsty. The lockets were full of magic fairy dust which the girls could use to take them to Fairyland if ever they needed help from the fairies.

"Thanks for asking me to stay," said Kirsty, cutting another piece of ribbon. "Mum says she and Dad will collect me on Christmas Eve."

"We might get some snow before then!" Rachel smiled. "The weather's getting much colder. I wonder what Christmas is like in Fairyland . . ."

At that moment, the door opened and Mrs Walker came in. She was followed by Buttons, Rachel's friendly, shaggy dog. He was white with grey patches and a long, furry tail.

"Oh, girls, that looks lovely!" Rachel's mum exclaimed when she saw the cards hanging on the walls. "We'll go over to

Lakeland Farm and choose a Christmas
tree this evening."

"Hurrah!" said Rachel. "Can Kirsty
and I decorate it?"

"We were hoping you would!" her
mother laughed. "You'd better get the
decorations out of the garage after lunch."

"Buttons seems to love Christmas too,"
Kirsty said, smiling. The dog was sniffing
around the cards and ribbons.

"He does," Rachel replied. "Every year
I buy him some doggie treats and wrap
them up. And every year he finds them
and eats them before
Christmas!"

Buttons wagged
his tail. Then he
grabbed the end
of a ribbon in his

mouth, and ran off, trailing red ribbon
behind him.

"Buttons, no!" Rachel
yelled, and she and
Kirsty ran after him
to get the ribbon back.
When the girls had
finished hanging the Christmas cards,
it was time for a delicious lunch of hot
soup. Then Rachel took Kirsty out to the
garage to fetch the decorations.

"It's getting colder," Kirsty said,
shivering. "Maybe it will snow."

"I hope so," Rachel replied. She
switched the garage light on. "The
decorations are up there." She pointed at
a shelf above the workbench. "I'll stand
on the stepladder and hand the boxes
down to you."

"OK," Kirsty agreed.

Rachel climbed up the ladder, and began to lift the boxes down. They were full of silver stars, shiny tinsel and glittering baubles in pink, purple and silver.

"I hope you've got a fairy for the top of the tree!" Kirsty joked, as Rachel handed her a box.

"No, we don't!" Rachel laughed. "We've always had a silver star, but it's getting quite old and tatty now. Be careful, Kirsty," she went on, lifting another box from the shelf. "This one's got all sorts of things sticking out of it. Oh!" Rachel gasped with surprise. The gold locket around her neck had caught on a little sparkling wreath made of twigs. The locket burst open, scattering fairy dust all over both girls.

"Oh, no!" Rachel cried, scrambling down from the ladder.

"What shall we do?" Kirsty began.

But they didn't have time to do anything. Suddenly, both girls were caught up in a swirling cloud of fairy dust that swept them off their feet. The sparkles whirled around them, glittering in the pale winter light.

"Kirsty, we're shrinking!" Rachel cried. "I think we're on our way to Fairyland!"

Chapter Two
Christmas Chaos

The girls weren't scared because this had happened to them before. But, as they whirled through the clouds towards Fairyland, Rachel felt a bit embarrassed. She hadn't meant to use her magic fairy dust at all – it was an accident!

"Don't worry," called Kirsty, seeing the

look on Rachel's face. "It'll be lovely to see our fairy friends again."

Soon the girls spotted the red and white toadstool houses of Fairyland below them, and then the silver palace with its four pink turrets.

As the girls drifted closer to the palace, they could see a crowd of fairies waving at them. There was King Oberon and Queen Titania, with the Rainbow Fairies and all the Weather Fairies, too. Even Doodle, the fairy cockerel, had come to greet them.

"Hello!" called Ruby and Saffron.
"It's wonderful to see you!" cried Pearl
and Storm.

As the girls landed on the
ground, the fairies
crowded around
them.
Rachel
quickly tried
to explain.
"I'm sorry,"
she gasped.
"We didn't
mean to come.
It was an
accident."
The Queen smiled. "No,
it wasn't an accident!" she said
in her silvery voice. "Our magic

made your locket open. I'm afraid we
need your help again, girls!"

The two friends turned to stare at each
other in surprise, their eyes wide.

"Not Jack Frost again?" Kirsty asked.

"Hasn't he been banished to the end of
the rainbow?" Rachel added.

"We'll tell you all about it," replied the
Queen. "But first . . ."

She waved her wand
at Rachel's locket. It
filled with fairy dust
again, and closed,
all on its own.

"Now," the King
said, turning to the
fairies. "Where is Holly,
the Christmas Fairy?"

Kirsty and Rachel watched eagerly as
Holly came forward. They had never met
the Christmas Fairy before. She had long
dark hair, and she wore a little red dress,
exactly the same colour as a holly berry.
The dress had a hood with furry white
trim, and she wore tiny red boots. But
although she was the Christmas Fairy,
Holly looked rather sad.

"Holly is in charge of putting the

sparkle into Christmas," Queen Titania
explained.

"That's right," Holly sighed. "I organise
Santa's elves, and I teach the reindeer
to fly. It's my job to make sure that
Christmas is as sparkly and happy as
possible."

"But this year Jack Frost is causing

trouble," the King told them. "We let him come back from the end of the rainbow because he said he was sorry and he promised to behave."

"And we agreed that he could help Doodle with the wintry weather," said Queen Titania.

"So what happened?" Rachel asked.

"Well, Jack Frost sent a letter to Father Christmas asking for presents," the King went on. "But he got a letter back saying he'd been so naughty, he wouldn't be getting anything this year!"

"We'll show you what Jack Frost did next," said the Queen.

She waved her wand over a small pool of
blue water which lay amongst the flowers.
The water bubbled and fizzed, and then
became smooth as glass.

Pictures began to appear on the surface.
Kirsty and Rachel saw a large log cabin
at night-time. It was surrounded by deep
snow, and icicles hung from the wooden
roof. Inside, the cabin was full of toys.
There were dolls, jigsaws, bikes, games,
puzzles and books, all lying around in huge
heaps. Kirsty and Rachel had never seen

so many toys in one place.

"Oh!" Kirsty gasped, her hand flying to her mouth. "Rachel, look!"

In the corner of the cabin stood a beautiful wooden rocking-horse. Someone was painting gold patterns onto the rockers. He was all dressed in red and white, and he had a jolly face with a long white beard.

"It's Father Christmas!" Rachel cried happily.

Then the picture changed to show the

outside of the cabin again. There the girls could see Santa's sleigh. It was silver and white, and sparkled with magic. Eight reindeer were harnessed to the sleigh, all ready to go. They were waiting patiently, shaking their antlers every so often.

Lots of little elves wearing bright green tunics scurried around the sleigh, filling it with presents. The bells on the tips of their hats tinkled merrily as they rushed here and there with armfuls of parcels.

Kirsty and Rachel were so delighted,

they almost forgot why they were watching. But then, just as the sleigh was full to bursting with presents, the thin, spiky figure of Jack Frost appeared.

As Kirsty and Rachel watched, Jack Frost peeped out from behind the log cabin. When there were no elves near the sleigh, he ran over to it and jumped in. Grabbing the reins, he shouted a spell to make the reindeer obey him. And the next moment, the sleigh lifted off the ground and zoomed away into the starry night sky.

As soon as the elves saw what was happening, they gave chase, but the

magic sleigh was much too fast for them
to catch.

"Oh, how could
he?" Kirsty said
crossly. "He's stolen
Santa's sleigh!"

"So now you see why
we need your help," said Queen Titania,
as the pictures faded away. "Holly must
find Santa's sleigh and return it before
Christmas Eve, or Christmas will be
ruined for all the children around the
world!"

"We think Jack Frost has taken the
sleigh to your world," Holly added. "He
loves parties, so he won't want to miss
Christmas. Will you help me?"

"Of course we will," Rachel and Kirsty
replied together.

Holly smiled. "Thank you!" she cried, giving both girls a hug.

"Where should we start looking?" asked Rachel.

"As always, the magic will come to you," Titania said with a smile. "You'll know when you are on the right track. And Holly will help. But there is one more thing you need to know…" The Queen waved her wand over the pool once more, and the girls watched as an image of three presents appeared. They were wrapped in beautiful golden paper, and tied with big

bows that glittered in all the colours of
the rainbow.

"These three presents were on the sleigh
when Jack Frost took it and they are very
special," the Queen explained. "So please
try to find them."

"We'll do our best," said Kirsty, and
Rachel nodded.

The King stepped forward, holding a
soft golden bag. "This can help you to
defeat Jack Frost," he said, opening the
bag and showing the girls a sparkling
fairy crown. "It has powerful magic. If
Jack Frost puts it on, he will immediately

be brought here to appear
before Queen Titania
and me."

Kirsty took the
bag and put the
strap safely over her shoulder.

"Good luck, Rachel and Kirsty!" called
the Queen. She raised her wand and sent
another shower of fairy dust whirling
and swirling around the girls. Rachel and
Kirsty were lifted off their feet to begin
the journey home.

Chapter Three
Buttons on the Loose!

"We're back!" Rachel said, as the sparkling clouds of fairy dust cleared. They were in the Walkers' garage again.

"And we're back to normal size," Kirsty added, brushing a speck of fairy dust from her jeans. "Poor Holly. I hope we can help."

"We'll find mean old Jack Frost!" said Rachel. "But we'd better take these decorations inside now. Mum will be wondering where we've been."

Kirsty popped the tiny golden bag into her pocket for safekeeping. Then she helped Rachel carry the boxes into the house. There they started looking through the decorations.

"I see what you mean about the star," Kirsty said, holding up a large but tattered silver star.

"Maybe Mum will let me buy something new for the top of the tree," replied Rachel. "I'd love to have a fairy up there this year!"

The girls spent the afternoon sorting out the decorations. Rachel's dad arrived home from work at six o'clock, and then they all went to Lakeland Farm to choose the Christmas tree.

"It looks like everyone's had the same idea!" remarked Rachel's mum, as the car drew up outside the farm. Lots of people were looking at Christmas trees.

There seemed to be hundreds of them in all shapes and sizes.

"At least there are plenty of trees!" Kirsty laughed.

"And we'll find the perfect one," said Rachel, climbing out of the car.

The two girls hurried over to the farmyard, while Mr and Mrs Walker followed with Buttons. The evening was cold and clear, and stars glittered up in the dark sky.

"Don't choose one that's too big," called Mrs Walker. "We'll never get it through the front door."

Rachel and Kirsty wandered up and down the rows of trees. But they couldn't seem to find one which was just right. They were either too big, too small, too bushy or too thin.

Then Rachel's eye was caught by one tree just ahead of her. The needles were so green and shiny, they almost seemed to glow in the frosty air. "That tree looks perfect," she said to herself, as she went over to it. "It's not too big and it's not too small." Suddenly, Rachel spotted a bright red glow, right in the middle of the tree. Then a tiny face peeped out at her.

"It's me!" Holly cried, waving her wand and sending little sparkly red holly berries bouncing over the tree.

Rachel laughed. "Kirsty, over here!" she called.

Kirsty rushed over. "What are you doing here, Holly?" she asked. "Is Jack Frost close by?"

But before Holly could answer, there was a shout from Mrs Walker, and Buttons dashed past the girls, his lead trailing along behind him. He was barking loudly.

"Stop him, girls!" puffed Mrs Walker. "I don't know what's the matter with him. He pulled the lead right out of my hand."

"We'll catch him, Mum," Rachel called. "You look after our tree."

Holly hopped inside Kirsty's pocket, and then the girls ran after the excited dog. Buttons had left the farmyard, and was racing towards an oak tree. Suddenly,

Kirsty saw a shadow dodge out from
behind the tree, and head for an old
barn. Although it
was dark, she could
just about make out
a sharp, pointed nose
and big feet.

"Oh!" she gasped,
"I think Buttons is
chasing one of Jack
Frost's goblins!"

"I knew they
were round here
somewhere!" Holly cried. "Quick! After
him!"

Buttons was standing outside the barn,
sniffing at the door.

"The goblin must be inside," Rachel
whispered, grabbing the dog's lead.

Quickly she hooked it
over a nail sticking out
of the barn wall, and
gave him a pat. "Wait
here quietly, Buttons," she
whispered. "We won't be
long."

"Let's look inside," Kirsty said. She
edged the barn door open and they all
peeped in. A cold blast of icy air swirled
around them. The girls and Holly could
see across the barn to the large doors at
the opposite end. Those doors were wide
open, and a sparkling trail led out of the
barn and right up into the sky. At the far
end of the trail, they could make out a
glittering silver shape travelling very fast.
It was Santa's missing sleigh!

Chapter Four
Grumpy Goblins

"Jack Frost was here," Kirsty said, looking disappointed. "We've just missed him."

"That's why it's so cold," Holly agreed with a shiver.

The barn was full of bales of straw, and looking around, Rachel noticed that there was wrapping paper scattered all over them. "Jack Frost has been opening Santa's presents!" she said crossly. "Isn't he mean?"

"Ssh!" Holly whispered. "Goblins!"

Two goblins had just rolled out from behind one of the straw bales near the open doors. They were fighting and yelling at each other.

"It's mine!" shouted one with a wart on his nose.

"No, it's mine!" yelled the other.

"Look," Rachel said. She pointed at the present the goblins were arguing over. "It's one of the three special presents the

Queen asked us to look for!"

"We must get that back," said Holly.

"The other two presents must still be on the sleigh," Kirsty added. "I don't see any more of that special gold wrapping paper anywhere about."

The goblins were still fighting, rolling around on the dusty floor of the barn trying to snatch the present from each other.

"Give it to me!" yelled the warty goblin. "There might be Christmas cake inside, or brandy snaps, or scrummy mince pies, or—"

"Mince pies!" the other goblin cried,

licking his lips. "I'm going to eat them all!"

"What are we going to do?" Rachel whispered. "How are we going to get the present back?"

Kirsty frowned. "I've got an idea," she said. "That goblin seems to like mince pies. Holly, could you magic up the smell of them?"

Holly's eyes twinkled. "Of course," she replied.

"We'll tell the goblins there's a big plate of mince pies in the hayloft," Kirsty went on. "They're so greedy, they're bound to go and look. And they can't climb the ladder and hang on to the parcel. We'll be able to grab it!"

Rachel and Holly beamed at her.

"Great idea!" said Holly. "One magic smell of hot mince pies coming up!" And she flew towards the goblins.

Chapter Five
Holly's Magic Trick

Rachel and Kirsty watched anxiously as Holly fluttered over the goblins' heads. They were so busy fighting, they didn't notice her.

Holly waved her wand in the air, and a few seconds later the smell of freshly-baked mince pies began to waft around the barn. Even Rachel and Kirsty who were standing outside could smell it.

The goblins stopped fighting. They lifted their big noses into the air and sniffed hard.

"Fresh mince pies!" Holly called, and she pointed at the ladder to the hayloft. "Up in the hayloft. Help yourselves."

"Mince pies! Yum!" shouted one of the goblins. He shoved the present at the other one, and dashed for the ladder. But the other goblin didn't want to be left behind. He raced over to the ladder too, hot on his friend's heels. As soon as he realised that he couldn't climb up to the hayloft with the present in his arms, he threw it down on a pile of straw.

Rachel and Kirsty laughed to themselves, as they watched the goblins scrambling up the ladder and trying to shove each other out of the way. When they had reached the top, the girls dashed into the barn and Kirsty picked up the

golden parcel.

Suddenly there was a shout from above.
"There aren't any mince pies here! We've
been tricked!"

One of the goblins peered down into
the barn. "Where's that tricksy little
Christmas fairy?" he yelled.

"Quick!" gasped Holly, "Let's get out of
here!"

The girls and Holly dashed for the door
as the goblins tumbled down the ladder.
"After them!" the first goblin shouted.

Outside the barn Rachel fumbled to
free Button's lead from
the nail. The goblins
appeared in the
doorway and ran
towards her. But Buttons
began to bark loudly as
soon as he saw them.
The goblins looked wary.

"You get the present back!" the first
goblin yelled, nudging the other.

"No, you get it!" his friend shouted.

Still barking, Buttons began pulling
Rachel towards them. Immediately, the
two terrified goblins shot back into the
barn and shut the door.

"Good dog!" said Rachel, patting
Buttons to calm him down. Meanwhile,
Kirsty showed the present to Holly.

"Hurrah! We've found one special present," Holly beamed. "I'll get this back to Fairyland right away." She waved her wand over the gift and in a magic cloud of sparkling red holly berries, the present disappeared back to Fairyland.

"We'll see you again soon," Rachel called, as Holly fluttered up into the sky.

"I'll be back as soon as I find out where Jack Frost is now!" Holly promised.

Rachel and Kirsty hurried back to the farmyard to find Mr and Mrs Walker. They had bought the tree that Rachel had chosen, and were tying it securely to the roof of the car.

"Now, I think it's time we all went home and had some mince pies and hot chocolate," said Rachel's mum, as they climbed into the car.

Rachel and Kirsty grinned at each other.

"Mince pies would be lovely, Mum," said Rachel, trying not to laugh.

"I think Buttons deserves a mince pie too," Kirsty whispered. "After all, he was the one who led us to the goblins and the first present."

"Woof!" Buttons agreed.

"Yes, and our fairy adventures aren't over yet," Rachel said, her eyes shining. "We'll save the sleigh and then this will be the best Christmas ever!"

Story Two
A Narrow Escape

Chapter Six
Christmas Shopping

"Two days till Christmas!" Rachel said the next morning, as she stood in front of the bedroom mirror, brushing her hair. The girls were getting ready to go Christmas shopping with Rachel's mum. "Isn't it exciting, Kirsty?"

Kirsty nodded. "I can't wait!" she said.

"But I don't want it to arrive too soon. We have to find Jack Frost and Santa's sleigh first."

"I know," Rachel agreed. "Once we've helped our fairy friends, then we can really start to enjoy Christmas."

"I need to buy a present for my mum," Kirsty went on. "Have you got many presents left to buy?"

Rachel shook her head. "Only one," she replied. "But the shopping centre has fantastic Christmas displays, so it's fun to look around even if you haven't got much shopping to do."

"Girls, are you ready yet?" Mrs Walker

called up the stairs.

"Coming, Mum," Rachel yelled back.

The girls clattered downstairs, laughing and chatting. Mrs Walker was waiting for them in the hall. "Don't forget your scarves and gloves," she said, picking up her car keys. "It's absolutely freezing today, and the shopping centre car park is outside."

She opened the front door, and went to get the car from the garage.

Rachel shivered as a blast of cold air swept through the open door, and rustled through the tinsel on the Christmas tree.

"Brr!" she gasped, grabbing her coat. "Mum's right. It is cold today."

"Doesn't the tree look fantastic?" said Kirsty admiringly, pulling on her gloves. The Walkers had a large entrance hall and they had put the tree in a corner

near the stairs. Rachel and Kirsty had decorated it beautifully, and now it glittered and gleamed with baubles, tinsel and toys.

"It's the nicest one we've ever had," Rachel agreed. "But I'll switch the lights off now we're going out."

Kirsty watched as Rachel switched off

the Christmas tree lights, and then she
noticed that something was different
about the tree. Instead of the tired
and tattered silver star which she had
carefully placed on the top, there now sat
a beautiful, sparkly fairy!

As Kirsty stared in surprise, she realised
that the fairy was a
real one. Holly was
perched at the top
of the tree, glowing
brightly in her
berry-red dress, and
waving at Kirsty.

"Holly!" Kirsty
laughed. "What
are you doing up
there?"

"I thought

your tree was missing a fairy!" Holly
grinned.

Rachel looked up to see Holly fly
down from the tree and land on Kirsty's
shoulder. "Hello, Rachel,"
sang Holly in her
pretty, tinkly voice.
"I have a feeling
something magical
is going to happen
today, so can I come
to the shops with
you?"

"Of course," Rachel
replied, happily. "But you'll
have to hide from my mum!"

"No problem." Holly winked at the
girls, and snuggled down inside Kirsty's
coat pocket, folding her wings away

neatly. She popped out a second later to say "Don't forget the magic crown!"

"It's in my pocket," Rachel assured her.

Then they heard Rachel's mum toot the car horn.

"Maybe something magical is going to happen!" Rachel whispered to Kirsty, as they rushed outside. "Maybe today

we'll get Santa's sleigh and the two
special presents back."

"I hope so!" Kirsty agreed with a smile.

Chapter Seven
A Chilling Suspicion

Although it was still early in the morning, the shopping centre was already busy when they arrived. Mrs Walker had to queue to get into the car park, and it took them quite a while to find an empty space.

"Now then, Rachel," she said, as they

all climbed out of the car, "would you and Kirsty like to go shopping on your own? I have some presents to buy which I don't want you to see!"

"Like what?" Rachel asked curiously.

Her mum laughed. "If I tell you, then they won't be a surprise, will they?" she said. "We'll split up, and I'll meet you and Kirsty in an hour by the glass lifts. Make sure you stay inside the shopping centre."

"OK," the girls agreed.

Mrs Walker went to get the lift, while the girls stayed on the ground floor. They walked through the shopping centre,

looking at the Christmas displays in the
shop windows and chatting happily.
Christmas songs were playing over the
speaker system, and people were bustling

to and fro carrying lots of shopping bags.
Rachel and Kirsty had soon bought the
few presents they had left to get. Kirsty
bought some pretty silver earrings for her
mum, and Rachel bought a dark green

diary for her dad.

"Are you OK in there, Holly?" Kirsty
whispered, putting the earrings into her
other pocket.

Holly nodded. She
was peeping out from
Kirsty's pocket to see
what was going on.
But she was so small,
nobody noticed her amongst the hustle
and bustle.

"Come and see the Christmas display,"
Rachel said to Kirsty. "It's beautiful."

Kirsty nodded eagerly, and Rachel led
the way to the big central square of the
shopping centre. There, right in front of
them, was Santa's Grotto.

"Wow!" said Kirsty, her eyes wide.
"This is fantastic!"

The grotto was a huge white tent covered in sparkling lights that changed colour from white to blue to silver and then back again. Long, glittering icicles hung from the roof. The tent was surrounded by fake snow, and there were life-size toy polar bears and penguins that waved at the shoppers. Near the tent was a small ice rink. Boys and girls dressed as elves were skating to and fro, some carrying brightly-wrapped parcels, others performing acrobatics and tumbles. A

pretty little bridge made of sparkling icicles
led the way into the grotto.

"Isn't it lovely?" Rachel said, as they
moved closer to get a better look.

There was a long queue of children
waiting to see Santa. Rachel and Kirsty
were standing near the bridge, watching
the elves on the ice rink, when a little girl
ran out of the grotto to join her mum.
She seemed upset and Kirsty and Rachel
couldn't help overhearing what she said.

"Did you have a good time, darling?" the mother asked.

"Well, Santa's sleigh was all bright and sparkly," the little girl told her breathlessly, "and his reindeer were furry and friendly. But Santa wasn't very nice!" She stuck her bottom lip out as if she was about to cry. "He wouldn't let me have a present, even though he had lots and lots. And he was all cold and spiky!"

Immediately Rachel's ears pricked up. That didn't sound like Santa at all. But it did sound like someone else she knew – someone mean and tricky and cunning. Rachel thought they might just have found Jack Frost!

Chapter Eight
Not the Real Santa!

"Kirsty!" Rachel said, pulling her friend to one side so their conversation wouldn't be overheard. "Did you and Holly hear that? I think Jack Frost might be inside the grotto, pretending to be Santa!"

Kirsty stared at Rachel. "You could be right!" she gasped.

"Yes," Holly piped up. "We'd better check it out."

"How are we going to get into the tent?" asked Rachel. "It'll take ages if we have to queue."

"She's right," Kirsty said. "Let's try and slip in round the back and see what's going on."

The girls crept round the back of the grotto, keeping a sharp eye out for anyone who might try to stop them. But they found the tent was tied down so firmly, they couldn't sneak underneath.

"Leave this to me!" Holly

whispered. She waved her wand, and a
shower of sparkling red
fairy dust fell onto a
corner of the tent.
Immediately the
ropes loosened,
and that part of
the canvas
curled upwards.
   "Thanks,
Holly!" said
Rachel. "Come
on, Kirsty."
   The two girls crept
cautiously under the edge of the tent
and into the grotto. Inside were lots of
glittering ice-covered rocks. Rachel,
Kirsty and Holly hid behind them while
they looked around.

The grotto was lit with magical, rainbow-coloured lanterns which glowed in the dim interior. Long, gleaming icicles hung from the ceiling, and a big Christmas tree stood in one corner, decorated with shiny silver baubles and multi-coloured fairy lights.

Kirsty shivered. The air inside the tent felt frosty. "It's really chilly in here," she whispered. "Jack Frost must be nearby."

And sure enough, there, in the middle
of the room was Santa's beautiful
sparkling sleigh, complete with hundreds
of presents, eight magic reindeer and
Jack Frost! He was ripping open a parcel,
although the ground in front of him was
already littered with discarded wrapping
paper. He wore a red Santa suit and a
big fake white beard. But he still looked
his mean, cold spiky self.

"Bring me another!" he roared, tossing aside the game of Snakes and Ladders he'd just opened.

His goblin servants came rushing from every corner of the grotto. They were all carrying parcels, which they pushed into Jack Frost's greedy hands. Rachel and Kirsty held their breath nervously as goblins hurried past their hiding place.

Suddenly Kirsty spotted something.
"Look!" she hissed, pointing at the sleigh.
"It's one of the special
presents!"

The shiny,
gold-wrapped
parcel was
sitting at the
back of the sleigh,
on top of a pile of
other toys.

"You're right," Holly
whispered excitedly. "And the
third one must still be on the sleigh
somewhere, too. It doesn't look as though
Jack Frost has already opened it."

"But however are we going to get
hold of them without Jack Frost and his
goblins spotting us?" Rachel asked.

"If we keep behind the rocks, we can crawl round to the back of the sleigh without being seen," said Kirsty.

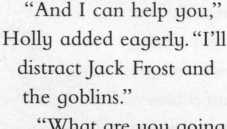

"And I can help you," Holly added eagerly. "I'll distract Jack Frost and the goblins."

"What are you going to do?" asked Kirsty

"I'll magic myself inside one of the presents that Jack Frost is opening," Holly replied. "That'll give him a shock!"

"That's a great idea," Rachel declared. "Now, we'll creep up to the back of the sleigh. Then, while Holly creates a diversion, you grab the present, Kirsty, and I'll try to drop the magic crown on Jack Frost's head."

"OK. Let's go," Kirsty whispered.

Holly nodded. She waved
her wand above her
head and immediately
disappeared.

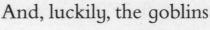

Rachel and Kirsty
began to crawl on their
hands and knees towards
the sleigh, keeping out of sight behind
the rocks. Jack Frost was far too busy
unwrapping presents to notice them.

And, luckily, the goblins
were preoccupied
with running
backwards and
forwards,
trying to keep
their grumpy
master happy.

Their hearts thumping, the girls drew nearer to the sleigh. The special present was so close now that Kirsty could reach out and touch it.

"Now we just wait for Holly to make her move," Rachel whispered.

The girls watched Jack Frost ripping the paper off yet another parcel. "I'm bored," he grumbled coldly. "Why can't I get a really nice present?" He threw the paper on the floor, and held up a pretty wooden box. "I wonder what's in here?" he muttered.

Suddenly the lid
of the box burst
open. Holly shot
out in a huge
shower of glittering
red holly berries
and fairy dust,
making Jack Frost
and the goblins
cough and splutter.

"This is our chance!" Kirsty said to
Rachel, as Jack Frost and his goblins
stared at Holly in stunned surprise.

Rachel nodded and together the girls
moved towards Jack Frost.

Chapter Nine
The Chase is On ...

Kirsty stretched out her hand for the
special parcel. Meanwhile, Rachel pulled
the crown out of her pocket, and stood up,
ready to drop it onto the fake Santa's head.

"What's going on?" Jack Frost shouted,
still rubbing fairy dust out of his eyes.
"It's that pesky Christmas Fairy, isn't it?

Grab her, goblins!"

Kirsty had her hands on the parcel now, and Rachel was leaning over the sleigh with the crown. But just then, one of the goblins spotted her. "Look out!" he screeched, pointing at Rachel.

Jack Frost spun round. His cold, hard eyes met Rachel's and she felt herself shiver. Quickly, Jack Frost waved his wand, and immediately the reindeer galloped off, pulling the sleigh behind them. Luckily, Kirsty was still hanging on to the ribbon of the parcel.

As the sleigh moved away, the present tumbled off the back and fell safely into her arms.

"I want you to grab that fairy!" Jack Frost roared at his goblin servants as the reindeer galloped towards the tent entrance, taking the sleigh with them. "And those interfering girls, too!"

"Kirsty! Rachel!" shouted Holly, who was zooming up and away from the goblins. "You've got to get out of here!"

The reindeer galloped out of the
tent and flew up into the air above the
shoppers. As the sleigh soared overhead,
the shoppers looked up in amazement.
They gasped, and then began clapping
and cheering, thinking it was some sort
of fabulous Christmas magic show.

The sleigh flew through the shopping centre and out of the big double doors. Meanwhile, the goblins were closing in on the girls, backing them into a corner of the tent. "We've got you now!" one of them snarled.

"You can't get the better of us!" boasted another.

Kirsty and Rachel felt very scared. "Split up and run for it, when I give the word!" Rachel whispered. She waited until the goblins were quite close, and then shouted, "Now!"

Immediately, she and Kirsty ran as fast
as they could in opposite directions. The
goblins chased after them, but there was a
lot of pushing and shoving and shouting
as the clumsy goblins bumped into each
other and tripped over their own feet.

In the middle of the chaos, Rachel and Kirsty both headed for the doorway. Kirsty reached it first. She noticed that Rachel was nearly at the exit, too, but a goblin was very close behind her, and as Kirsty slipped out of the tent, she saw the goblin make a grab for her friend!

Chapter Ten
The Great Escape

The goblin missed Rachel and fell over, tripping up another goblin who was hot on his heels. The girls had escaped from the grotto, but they knew that the goblins were right behind them. They had hardly any time to get away.

"Quick, Kirsty!" Rachel shouted.

"Those support ropes at the back of the
tent – we need to pull them out!"

Kirsty knew exactly what Rachel had
in mind. The two girls began pulling at
the ropes with all their might.

Suddenly there was a creaking sound
and the ropes gave way. The large white
tent wobbled a little and then
fell to the ground, trapping the goblins
underneath the heavy white canvas.

"We did it!" Kirsty gasped. "Well done,
Rachel. That was a brilliant idea!"

"Yes, but I think we'd better get out of here before those goblins escape," Rachel whispered. "It's almost time to meet Mum anyway."

"Where's Holly?" asked Kirsty, looking around.

"Here I am!" called a tiny, silvery voice, and Holly zoomed over to land on Kirsty's shoulder. All the shoppers were too busy staring at the collapsed tent to notice the tiny fairy.

"Are you all right?" Rachel asked anxiously.

"I'm fine," Holly beamed. "Thank you for getting the

second present. The Fairy King and
Queen will be pleased!"

Kirsty held the parcel out and Holly
waved her wand over it. Fairy dust
fluttered down around it and the present
promptly vanished back to Fairyland.

"I almost got the crown on Jack Frost's head!" Rachel sighed, as she placed it carefully back into her pocket. "But he got away again. And we don't know where he's gone."

"Oh, yes, we do!" Holly told her excitedly. "While you were escaping from the goblins, I followed the sleigh and spoke to one of my reindeer friends."

"What did he say?" asked Rachel eagerly.

"He told me Jack Frost is really annoyed that we keep finding him in the human world," Holly explained.

"He wants to open all of Santa's presents in peace and quiet. So he's told the reindeer to take him to his Ice Castle right away."

"His Ice Castle!" Kirsty exclaimed. "Is that where Jack Frost lives?"

Holly nodded.

"Do you know where it is, Holly?" Rachel asked.

"Yes," Holly replied. "It's a cold, scary place, but I can take you there tomorrow, if you still want to help?"

"Of course we do!" said Kirsty and Rachel together.

Holly beamed at them. "Then I'll whizz
back to Fairyland now and report to the
King and Queen," she went on. "Can
you get me out of this
shopping centre?"

"Of course," Kirsty
said, smiling. While
Holly hid under
Kirsty's scarf, the girls
walked quickly over to
one of the doors that led out into the car
park. When nobody was looking, Holly
slipped out from under the scarf, gave the
girls a cheery wave and then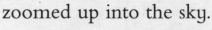
zoomed up into the sky.
The girls watched her
fly away until she
was out of sight.
Then they hurried

back through the shopping centre towards
the glass lifts, where they had promised to
meet Rachel's mum.

Mrs Walker was already waiting for
them, holding lots of
exciting-looking
carrier bags.

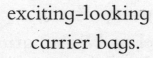

"Hello, girls,"
she smiled.
"I thought
you'd got lost!
Did you get
everything
you wanted?"
"Almost!"
Rachel replied,
with a quick glance
at Kirsty.
"Well, did you see

Santa's grotto?" Mrs Walker went on,
leading the way back to the car. "I
heard it was very beautiful – until it
collapsed! But some of the parents were
complaining that Father Christmas was
rather grumpy."

Rachel and Kirsty grinned at each
other. "He was!" Kirsty agreed.

"I wonder what's going to happen

tomorrow, Rachel," Kirsty whispered, as Mrs Walker unlocked the car. "Jack Frost's Ice Castle sounds scary."

"I know," Rachel whispered back. "But we can't let our fairy friends down."

"No," Kirsty agreed firmly. "We have to get Santa's sleigh and the third present."

"And this time we'll get that magic crown on Jack Frost's head!" added Rachel.

The girls exchanged a determined smile and climbed into the car, feeling very excited and a little bit nervous about just what tomorrow might have in store!

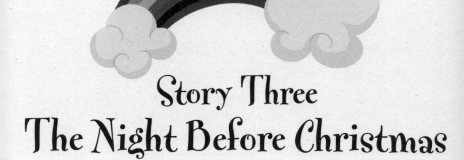

Story Three
The Night Before Christmas

Chapter Eleven
Winter Wonderland

Rachel opened her eyes and yawned.
She sat up in bed and looked across
at Kirsty, who was still asleep. "It's
Christmas Eve!" Rachel said to
herself excitedly. But it would only
be a merry Christmas if they
managed to get Santa's sleigh and

all the presents back to Santa today.
If they didn't, greedy Jack Frost would
spoil everything.

Rachel pushed back the duvet and
shivered. Even though the central heating
was on, there was still a chill in the air.
She went across to the window and
looked outside. "Oh!" she gasped.

It had snowed heavily during the
night, and the trees, the lawn and the
flowerbeds were all hidden under a thick

blanket of sparkling white snow.

"What is it?" Kirsty yawned.

"Sorry, did I wake you?" asked Rachel.
"I was just so surprised
to see the snow."

"Snow!" Kirsty
gasped. She jumped
out of bed and
ran over to join
Rachel. They
both peered out
of the frosty
window.

"It looks like
we're going to have a white Christmas,"
Rachel smiled.

"It'll be the best Christmas ever," Kirsty
agreed. "As long as we make it back from
Jack Frost's Ice Castle…"

"Are you scared?" asked Rachel.

"A bit," Kirsty replied. "But I'm not giving up. Are you?"

"No way!" Rachel laughed. "Come on. Let's get dressed and have breakfast. Then we can go outside."

The two girls hurried downstairs for scrambled eggs and toast. Then they pulled on their coats and boots, and ran out into the garden. Their feet sank into the soft snow, leaving tracks all over the lawn. It started snowing again, and pretty snowflakes drifted down all around them.

Kirsty rolled a snowball in her hands. "Let's have a snowball fight!" she grinned, and threw it at Rachel.

Laughing, Rachel ducked, but before the snowball reached her, it exploded in the air like a firework. Tiny sparkling icicles of red fire shot in all directions. As Kirsty and Rachel watched in amazement, Holly burst out of the snowball.

"Here I am!" she cried, shaking snowflakes from her red dress. " Are you ready, girls? It's time to go to Jack Frost's Ice Castle!"

Chapter Twelve
The Ice Castle

"We're ready!" Rachel said bravely.

Kirsty nodded and checked her pocket to make sure she had the magic crown.

Then Holly waved her wand in the air. Berry-red fairy dust drifted down over the girls, and they began to shrink. In a moment, they were fairy-sized with thin, gauzy wings on their backs.

Holly fluttered up into the air, and Rachel and Kirsty followed her.

"Here we go, then!" Holly said, waving her wand again.

It was snowing quite heavily now, and the falling snowflakes began to spin and dance around the girls until Rachel and Kirsty couldn't see anything at all.

Then, the blizzard of snow cleared as quickly as it had begun. Rachel and Kirsty gasped. They were no longer in the Walkers' back garden. Instead, they were sitting in a tree, staring up at Jack Frost's Ice Castle.

The castle stood on a tall hill, under a gloomy, grey winter sky. It was built from sheets of ice, and it had four towers tipped with icy blue turrets. The ice glittered and gleamed like diamonds, but the palace still looked cold and scary.

127

"Be careful," Holly whispered, as a couple of goblins wandered underneath the tree. "There are goblins everywhere. We'll never get in through the main gate."

"Maybe we can find another way in," Rachel suggested, looking upwards.

"Good idea," Holly replied. "Follow me." The girls followed Holly as she flew up towards one of the ice-blue turrets. "See what I mean?" Holly said quietly. Rachel and Holly peered down at the castle beneath them. Holly was right. There were goblin guards on every door.

"Maybe we can find
an open window,"
whispered Rachel.

Holly nodded. "Let's
split up and take a look.
We'll meet back here

in a few minutes."
They flew off in
different directions.
Kirsty went to look
around the tops of
the icy towers, one by

one. There
were lots of windows,
but all of them were
locked. She flew back to
meet Rachel and Holly.
Rachel was already

waiting. "I didn't have any luck," she
sighed. "Did you?"

Kirsty shook her head sadly.

At that moment, Holly fluttered down
to join them.

"You were a long time," said Kirsty.

"I had to hide from one of the goblins,"
Holly explained. "He was marching
along the battlements on guard duty."

"We didn't find any open windows,"

Rachel told her. "Did you?"

Holly shook her head. "No, but I found another way in!" she grinned. "Follow me!"

Holly led the girls to a place on the battlements and pointed at the icy floor. "Look!" she said.

"A trapdoor!" Kirsty gasped.

Holly nodded. "When I was hiding from the goblin, I saw him lift the trapdoor and go into the castle," she told them. "And I don't think he bolted it on the other side."

They checked that there were no

131

goblins around, and then flew down to the trapdoor. It was a slab of ice with a steel ring in the top.

"It looks very heavy," Rachel said with a frown.

"That's no problem," Holly said, smiling. She waved her wand and the trapdoor suddenly flew open in a whirl of fairy dust.

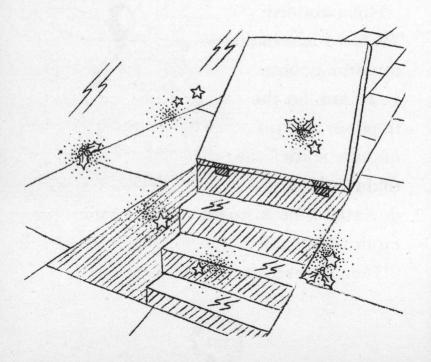

Below were steps
of ice, leading down
into the castle.
Shivering with cold,
Rachel, Kirsty
and Holly
flew inside.

"We must start
looking for Santa's
sleigh right away,"
Holly whispered to
the girls.

"It's not easy to hide a sleigh and eight
reindeer!" said Rachel thoughtfully.

"Maybe they're in the stables?" Kirsty
suggested.

"That's a good place to start," said
Holly. "But keep a sharp lookout for
goblins on the way!"

The friends flew down the winding staircase towards the ground floor of the castle. But as they fluttered round a corner of the stairs, they bumped straight into a goblin who was on his way up.

"Fairies!" roared the goblin furiously. "What are you doing here?" He grabbed at Holly, but missed as she darted out of reach. "Help! Fairies!"

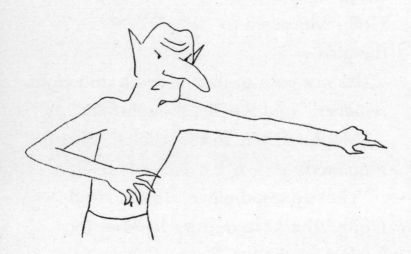

Holly, Rachel and Kirsty turned and whizzed back up the stairs. But as they reached the next corner, they heard the loud clatter of footsteps. Six more goblins rushed towards them!

Chapter Thirteen
Capture!

The friends tried to dodge out of the
way, but they were completely
surrounded by goblins. Holly and Rachel
were grabbed immediately. Kirsty tried
to fly away overhead, but one goblin
jumped onto another's shoulders and
caught hold of her ankle.

The goblins laughed gleefully. "Now you're our prisoners!" they gloated. "Jack Frost is going to be very pleased with us!"

The goblins took the friends through the Ice Castle and into the Great Hall. It was a huge room carved from shining sheets of ice. At one end was Jack Frost's throne. It looked very grand, made out of glittering icicles that had been twisted into shape.

But Jack Frost wasn't sitting on his throne. He was in Santa's sleigh! The reindeer were still harnessed to it, and they were feeding on bales of hay. Jack Frost was unwrapping more presents, and the floor was covered with wrapping paper and ribbons.

Rachel, Holly and Kirsty trembled as the goblins pushed them towards Jack Frost.

"Look what we've brought you!" one of the goblins called triumphantly.

Jack Frost looked up at the girls. "You again!" he snarled, staring at them with cold, hard eyes. "You're always trying to spoil my fun!"

He shook his fist, and Rachel gasped as she saw the present Jack Frost was holding in his other hand. He hadn't opened it yet. It was still wrapped in its pretty gold paper, and tied with a bow of rainbow colours. It was the third special present that the King and Queen of the fairies had asked the girls to find!

Rachel glanced at Kirsty and Holly. She could see that they'd spotted the present too. But how were they going to stop Jack Frost from opening it?

Kirsty was thinking the same thing as Rachel. She stared down at the piles of wrapping paper on the floor, and suddenly an idea struck her.

"What am I going to do with you?" Jack Frost was muttering, tapping his long, thin fingers on top of the present. "I think I'll put you in my deepest ice dungeon, and leave you there for one hundred years!"

"Rachel," Kirsty whispered. "I've got an idea. Can you distract the goblins and Jack Frost for a few moments?"

Rachel looked at her friend curiously, then nodded. "OK," she whispered back.

"Shall we take them to the dungeons, master?" asked one of the goblins.

"I haven't decided yet," Jack Frost snapped. "Now be quiet while I open this present." He lifted the parcel and shook it. "I can't wait to see what's inside!"

The goblins pressed forward, eager to

see what was inside the parcel too. The
goblin who was holding Rachel loosened
his grip slightly, and Rachel saw her
chance. She zoomed up into the air, then
flew straight for the door.

"Seize her!" Jack
Frost yelled furiously.

The goblins
rushed after
Rachel, shouting
instructions and
tripping over
each other's
feet.

Meanwhile,
Kirsty bent
down and
grabbed a piece
of silver wrapping

paper and a purple ribbon from the floor. While Jack Frost was watching the goblins, Kirsty pulled the gold bag with the magic crown in it out of her pocket and quickly wrapped it in the silver paper. Then she tied the ribbon around the parcel. Holly gave her a puzzled look. She had no idea what Kirsty was up to!

Jack Frost was getting more and more angry as his goblins failed to catch Rachel. Eventually, he waved his wand, and instantly Rachel's wings froze in mid-air. She fell to the ground, landing on top of two goblins.

"Now!" Jack Frost snapped, as two more goblins dragged Rachel to her feet. "I'm going to open this present!"

"Please, Your Majesty," said Kirsty, stepping forward. "May I say something?"

Jack Frost glared at her. "Make it quick!" he said crossly.

"Won't you take pity on us?" asked

Kirsty. "We only came here to get this one very special present." And she held up the crown, wrapped in silver paper. "It's for the Fairy King, you see, and it's very important. Won't you let us take it to him?"

Jack Frost's beady eyes lit up as he stared at the parcel Kirsty was holding. "A present for King Oberon?" he muttered. "Give it to me!"

"But—" Kirsty began.

"Now!" Jack Frost roared.

A goblin pushed Kirsty forward. Jack Frost dropped the present he was holding, and snatched the other one right out of Kirsty's hands.

Kirsty tried not to smile. She knew

greedy Jack Frost wouldn't be able to resist taking the Fairy King's present for himself! Now he was ripping the ribbon and paper away to reveal the golden bag. He put his hand inside and drew out the glittering crown.

"Aha!" he declared triumphantly. "It's a new crown! Well, I'll have that!" He lifted the crown and lowered it onto his frosty white hair.

Immediately, Jack Frost vanished!

Chapter Fourteen
A Magical Journey

The goblins gasped in surprise and fear.
They didn't know what had happened
to their master, and they thought they
might be next! They ran around the
Great Hall in panic. Some tried to hide
under the piles of wrapping paper, while
others huddled behind giant icicles.

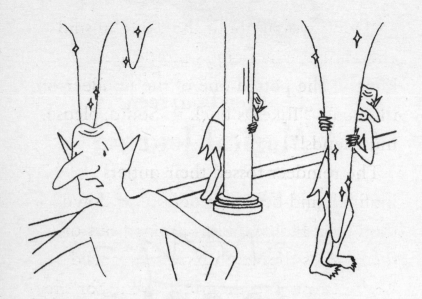

"Well done, Kirsty!" Holly laughed.

"Jack Frost's been sent straight to the Fairy King and Queen," cried Rachel in delight. She jumped into the magic sleigh and picked up the third present. "And it's time we were leaving, too!"

"But how are we going to get out of the castle?" asked Kirsty, as she hopped on board the sleigh.

"Don't worry about that," Holly said cheerfully. "The sleigh's magic, you know!" She patted one of the reindeer on the head. "Take us back to Santa, please, my friends!"

The reindeer tossed their antlers joyfully, and began to gallop off down the Great Hall. Goblins jumped out of the way as the sleigh picked up speed. Then it rose into the air, heading for the icy roof.

"Oh!" gasped Rachel. "We're going to crash!"

But, magically, the ice melted away as the sleigh approached, and soon the girls were soaring out of the castle, and up into the clouds. Then the reindeer raced across the sky so fast, that everything was a blur as the wind rushed quickly past the sleigh.

"Here's Santa's workshop!" Holly called at last.

The reindeer had slowed, and the sleigh was floating towards the ground. Rachel and Kirsty peered out eagerly. Below

them, they saw the pretty log cabin
which they had seen in the fairy pool.
And there was a large crowd of elves
outside, dancing in the snow, the bells on
their hats tinkling merrily.

"Hurrah!" they cried happily. "You've
found the sleigh and the
reindeer!" As the sleigh
landed, the elves ran
to pet the reindeer
and feed them
carrots.

Rachel and
Kirsty gasped
with delight as
Santa himself came
dashing out of the
cabin. He was in such a
hurry he hadn't even done up his coat.

"Welcome! Welcome!" Santa called, beaming all over his jolly face. "My beautiful sleigh and my precious reindeer are safe, thanks to you!"

"Are we in time to save Christmas, Santa?" Rachel asked anxiously.

Santa nodded. "Oh, yes," he smiled. "It's going to be a wonderful Christmas!"

"But what about the presents Jack

Frost opened?" Kirsty wanted to know. "Does that mean some children won't get anything?"

"Oh, no!" Santa boomed, looking quite shocked. "That would never do! My elves have made plenty of extra presents."

As he spoke, a group of elves ran out of the cabin, carrying armfuls of brightly-coloured gifts which they piled up in the magic sleigh.

"Now," said Santa, when the sleigh was full of presents once again. "The King and Queen will be wanting to see you. Come with me and I'll drop you off on my way to deliver these gifts."

Rachel and Kirsty climbed back into the sleigh looking thrilled. They were going to ride with Santa Claus on Christmas Eve!

Holly joined them, as Santa picked up the reins. "Let's go, my friends!" Santa called happily to the reindeer. "We have a lot of work to do today!"

Rachel and Kirsty grinned at each
other as the sleigh rose up into the sky
again and set off for Fairyland.

Chapter Fifteen
A Fairy Merry Christmas

As Santa's sleigh drew closer to
Fairyland, the girls and Holly could
see sparkling fireworks exploding below
them. Sweet music and the sound of
fairy laughter drifted up to the sleigh.

"There's a party at the palace," Holly
said. "They must have heard the news."

159

The reindeer swooped lower, and there was a shout of welcome from the fairies below as they spotted the sleigh. Rachel and Kirsty waved as they saw all their old friends waiting for them.

"Well done!" called King Oberon as the sleigh landed.

"You've helped Holly save Christmas!"
Queen Titania added.

The fairies cheered as Rachel, Kirsty
and Holly stepped out of the sleigh.

"We brought you this,"
Rachel said, handing
the third special
present to the King.

"Thank you!"
the King beamed.
"Won't you stay
and join the party,
Santa?"

Santa shook his
head. "I'd love to, but
I have a lot of work to
do!" he laughed. He shook
the reins. "Merry Christmas!"

"Merry Christmas!" everyone called, as

the silver sleigh flew out of sight.

"What's happened to Jack Frost?" asked Rachel.

The King looked stern. "He has had his magic powers taken away from him," he explained.

"And he must stay in his Ice Castle for a whole year before he is allowed to use magic again!" the Queen said. "But now it's time to celebrate Christmas, and we have special gifts for all three of you."

She clapped her hands, and two small fairies hurried forward. They carried the two special presents which Holly had brought back to Fairyland earlier.

"These presents are
particularly special
because they are for
the three of you!" the
Queen said.

Rachel, Holly and
Kirsty gasped in
surprise, and everyone
laughed.

"Since it's Christmas Eve,
you can open them right away," smiled
the King. And he handed Holly the
parcel that Rachel had just given him.

Eagerly Holly tore the gold paper off
the parcel, and peeped inside the box. "A
new wand!" she breathed. "It's beautiful!"

"It is extra sparkly and powerful,"
Queen Titania told her, as Holly twirled

the wand above her head. It left a trail of magic sparkles behind it, and made the sweet sound of tinkling Christmas bells.

"It will help you make Christmas more magical than ever before," said the Queen with a smile.

"Thank you, Your Majesty!" Holly beamed.

The Queen handed the other two presents to Rachel and Kirsty. They couldn't wait to see what was inside! Rachel managed to open hers a second before Kirsty, and she gasped with delight.

"It's a fairy doll!" Rachel said, her eyes shining. "Look, Kirsty — it's a fairy for the top of the Christmas tree!"

The doll sparkled and shone with magic. She wore a white dress which glittered with silver and gold, and a sparkling crown on her long hair. Kirsty had one exactly the same.

"I can't wait to get home and put it on our Christmas tree!" Kirsty said, smiling happily.

"There's just one more thing," the

Queen laughed. "These dolls are magic. Every year they will bring you a special Christmas present from the fairies!"

Rachel and Kirsty were thrilled to bits. They'd never expected this!

"But we mustn't keep you any longer," the King said suddenly. "It's time for you to go home, or you'll be late for Christmas!"

Quickly the girls said their goodbyes. They both had a special hug for Holly, and then the Queen waved her wand. "Thank you!" she called. "And Merry Christmas!"

"Merry Christmas!" Rachel and Kirsty replied, as

166

they were caught up in a whirl of magic fairy dust.

"Merry Christmas!" called all the fairies.

Suddenly the silvery fairy voices died away, the magic dust cleared, and Rachel and Kirsty found themselves back to their normal size in the Walkers' garden.

"We did it, Rachel!" Kirsty laughed breathlessly. "We saved Christmas!"

"Let's go inside and put my fairy doll on the Christmas tree," Rachel grinned.

The girls ran inside. Kirsty watched

as Rachel fixed the fairy doll carefully to the top of the tree.

"She looks lovely!" Rachel said happily.

Just then the doorbell rang. Rachel ran to see who it was, and found Kirsty's mum and dad standing on the doorstep outside.

"Merry Christmas!" said Mr and Mrs Tate with a big smile.

"Mum! Dad!" Kirsty cried, rushing over to them.

Mr and Mrs Tate stayed for tea and mince pies, and then it was time for Kirsty to leave. She gave Buttons a cuddle, and Rachel a hug.

"Have a great Christmas!" Kirsty told her friend.

"You too," Rachel replied. Then she stood on the doorstep with her mum and dad, waving at the Tates as they drove away.

Mr and Mrs Walker closed the front door and returned to the cosy living-

room, but Rachel stayed in the hall for a moment with Buttons. She stared up at the glittering fairy on top of the tree.

Then Rachel blinked hard. Was she seeing things? The fairy had smiled at her. And a cloud of magic sparkles had drifted from her wand!

Rachel looked down to see where the sparkles had fallen – and there was a present under the tree that hadn't been there before. It was wrapped in gold

paper and tied
with a bow that
glittered in all
the colours of the
rainbow.

Rachel smiled
and patted
Buttons. This really
was going to be
the best Christmas
ever!

The End

Jack Frost's Spell

Christmas mischief I have planned,
So, goblins, go to Fairyland!
Find the fairy Christmas tree
Bearing magic items – three.

Steal these special decorations
To spoil all Christmas celebrations.
Candle, Bauble, Magic Star —
Take them where no fairies are.

Stella the
Star fairy

Story One
The Magical Missing Candle

Chapter One
Darkness Falls

Mrs Tate popped her head round the door. "Are you ready, girls?" she asked. "It's time to leave for the Christmas Fair."

"Coming, Mum," Kirsty said, jumping up.

"I'm really glad I could come and visit," said Rachel Walker, as she followed her best friend into the hall to get their coats. Rachel had arrived at Kirsty's house after the last day of school term. Her parents were collecting her on Christmas Eve.

"Me too," Kirsty replied. "You're going to love the fair. And who knows . . . we might even see a Christmas fairy!"

Rachel and Kirsty thought they were the luckiest girls in the world because they had become friends with the fairies! Whenever the fairies were in trouble, they asked the girls for help – usually because cold, spiky Jack Frost was causing magical mayhem with the help of his nasty goblin servants.

"I forgot to tell you!" Kirsty said, pulling on her boots. "Every year someone from my school is chosen to be the fair's Christmas King or Queen, and this year it's my friend Molly."

"Wow! I bet she's really excited," said Rachel smiling.

"I'd love to be Christmas Queen!"

Kirsty nodded as her parents joined them.

"Everybody ready?" said Mrs Tate. "Then let's go . . ."

"Has someone turned the Christmas tree lights off?" Mr Tate asked. "They were on a few minutes ago, but they're off now."

Everyone shook their heads. Kirsty poked her head into the lounge where the tree stood.

"The switch at the wall is still on," she pointed out.

"The lights must be broken," Mr Tate decided. "Never mind, I'll fix them when we get back."

"Yes, we must go," Kirsty's mum agreed. "The parade starts soon."

Quickly, they left the house and walked up Twisty Lane towards the high street and Wetherbury Market Square.

"I can hear music," Rachel said, looking excited.

Although it was a cold, frosty night, the square was packed with people bustling around stalls selling brightly-painted tree decorations, Christmas crackers, cakes and gifts. There was even an old musical organ playing a merry tune.

"It's great, isn't it?" Kirsty said, her eyes shining. She pointed at a raised platform in the middle of the square. The Mayor of Wetherbury, in his splendid robe and gold chain, was standing there next to a large switch. "And it'll be even better when the Christmas Queen turns on the illuminations," Kirsty added.

Rachel glanced around. She could

see dark shapes made of bulbs here and there above their heads, but it was hard to make out what the shapes were. She was looking forward to seeing them all lit up.

"Ooh, I can't wait to see Molly!" Kirsty exclaimed, as the parade began.

The first float that rumbled into the square was Santa's workshop, with elves making toys and Santa sitting on a

golden sleigh.

"Oh, look!" Rachel gasped, as another float came into view, carrying a huge papier-mâché Christmas pudding with a sprig of holly on top. Several more floats followed, all looking wonderfully colourful and Christmassy.

"Here's Molly," Kirsty said to Rachel as the final float appeared. "Doesn't she look pretty?"

Kirsty's friend was dressed in white
and silver. Her dress had a long full
skirt, scattered
here and there
with sparkling
snowflakes,
and she wore
a glittering silver
tiara on her head.
She sat on a
jewelled throne,
waving at the
crowds. Behind
her rose an ice
palace, decorated
with gleaming
icicles.

Rachel nudged
Kirsty.

"The Christmas Queen's palace is much prettier than Jack Frost's gloomy Ice Castle!" she whispered, and Kirsty nodded eagerly.

The float drew to a halt next to the platform, and the mayor helped Molly up the steps as the crowd clapped.

"I would like to wish everyone in Wetherbury a very merry Christmas!" Molly announced. And then she pulled the switch with a flourish.

The square lit up in a dazzling
blaze of colour as the light
bulbs sprang to life.
Everyone oohed
and aahed as they
gazed round at
the illuminations
above.

"This is
amazing!" Kirsty
breathed.

"It's beautiful,"
Rachel agreed.
There were
hundreds of
snowflakes in different
sizes strung on wires
overhead, and they
all glittered with rainbow-

coloured lights.

The Christmas Queen had come down from the platform now, and was waving at the two girls.

"Hi, there!" Molly called, her face glowing with excitement. "Did you like my float?"

"It was lovely!" Kirsty replied. "Molly, this is my friend, Rachel."

"Hi, Molly," said Rachel, admiring Molly's sparkling dress. "You look lovely."

"And these are definitely the best illuminations Wetherbury has ever had!"

Kirsty added.

But just then, one of the snowflakes above their heads began to flicker. And as the girls glanced upwards, every single one of the beautiful snowflake illuminations suddenly flickered and then went out.

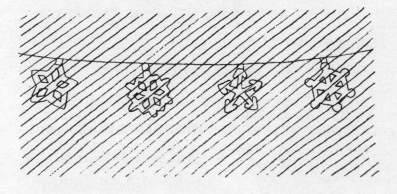

Chapter Two
Trouble in Fairyland

Everyone gasped in horror, including
the girls.

"What's happened?" asked Kirsty.
"They were fine a minute ago."

The mayor stood on the platform
and called for everyone's attention.
"Please don't worry," he said firmly,

"we'll soon have the lights fixed.
And in the meantime, enjoy the fair."

"It's a shame about the illuminations,"
Molly said, "but I've had a brilliant
evening!"

"I'm sure they'll be fixed by tomorrow,"
Kirsty replied.

"I hope so," Molly agreed. Then she
smiled at the girls.
"Now, I must go and
hand out presents
to the children who
were on the floats."
"A Christmas
Queen's work is
never done!" Kirsty
said with a grin.
Molly laughed
and waved as she

walked away towards the floats.

Rachel and Kirsty turned back to Mr
and Mrs Tate.

"What a pity the illuminations went
out," said Kirsty's mum. "They looked so
pretty."

"I'm glad I've only got to fix our tree
lights and not all these bulbs!" said Mr
Tate, smiling and shaking his head. "Let's
go home and get warm."

As Mr and Mrs
Tate walked on
ahead, Kirsty turned
to Rachel. "Isn't it
dark tonight? There
isn't a single star in
the sky—" Suddenly
she stopped dead,
clutching her friend's

arm. "Rachel, look!"

Rachel stared ahead. The high
street was lined with lamp posts
decorated with more of the snowflake
illuminations, and the one closest to the
girls contained a couple of light bulbs
that were shining brightly.

Kirsty looked puzzled. "How can those
bulbs be on, when all the others aren't

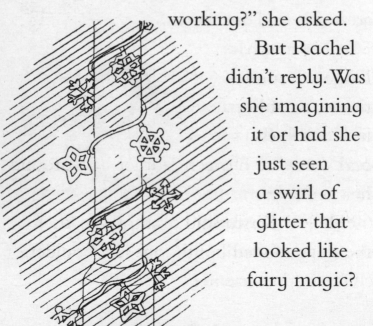

working?" she asked.

But Rachel
didn't reply. Was
she imagining
it or had she
just seen
a swirl of
glitter that
looked like
fairy magic?

"Rachel! Kirsty!" called a tiny, musical voice.

"It's a fairy!" Rachel gasped.

The fairy who was fluttering towards them, blonde ponytail bobbing, was dressed in Christmas green and red. A string of sparkly gold fairy lights was looped around the waist of her little red dress,  and she wore a green feather boa around her neck.

"Hello!" Kirsty said breathlessly, as the fairy landed lightly on her shoulder. "What's your name?"

"I'm Stella the Star Fairy," the fairy explained. "I'm in charge of all the sparkly Christmas illuminations, the fairy lights on Christmas trees and the stars that guide Santa and his reindeer on Christmas night!"

"Were you trying to turn the bulbs back on?" asked Rachel curiously.

Stella's delicate, gauzy wings drooped as she hung her head.

"I was," she sighed. "But look!"

The girls glanced up at the lamp post.

The bulbs which Stella had turned on had now gone out again.

"That's what happens every single time," Stella said glumly. "I turn a bulb on, but it just goes out!"

"Don't worry, Stella," said Kirsty
comfortingly. "They'll be fixed
tomorrow."

But Stella shook her head. "No, you
don't understand, Kirsty," she replied.
"This is all Jack Frost's fault!"

"Jack Frost?" Kirsty repeated, glancing
at Rachel. "Is he trying to spoil
Christmas again?"

"Yes," sighed Stella. "You see, every year at Christmas-time we have a huge Christmas tree in Fairyland. There are three very special and magical decorations on it, but wicked Jack Frost sent his goblin servants to steal them, and now they're gone!"

"Oh, no!" Kirsty said. "Why are these decorations so special?"

"The first one is the shining white candle," replied Stella. "It controls all the Christmas illuminations in the human world."

"So that's why the Wetherbury illuminations went out!" Rachel exclaimed.

Stella nodded. "The second is the glittering bauble. That controls all the Christmas tree fairy lights," she went on.

"Our tree lights!" Kirsty gasped. "That's why they're not working."

"And the third is the shining star from the top of the tree," Stella continued. "The star makes sure that the real stars shine in the night sky, to guide Santa when he's delivering presents. So we have to get all three of the decorations back from the goblins or Christmas will be ruined!"

"Do you know where the decorations are?" Kirsty asked.

"Well, when we realised what the goblins were doing, we chased them,"

explained Stella. "So only the goblin
with the magic star made it back to
Goblin Grotto. The others were forced
to flee into the human world, taking the
magic candle and bauble with them."

"Can we help find them?" asked
Rachel.

Stella beamed at her. "I was hoping
you'd say that!" she declared.
"The candle and the
bauble became
bigger when they
entered the human
world, so they're big
enough for you to
spot."

"Then we'll look
out for them," said
Rachel in a determined voice. "We won't

let Jack Frost spoil Christmas!"

"Thank you, girls!" cried Stella happily.
"I'll rush back to Fairyland and tell the
King and Queen that you're helping.
Remember not to search too hard – the
fairy magic will come to you!" And with
a wave of her glittering wand, Stella flew
away into the night.

Chapter Three
Carols and Candles

"There isn't much time before
Christmas," Rachel remarked, as
she finished her cereal the following
morning. "I hope we can get the candle,
the bauble and the star back by then."

"We'll do our best," Kirsty replied.
"Mum says we can go Christmas

shopping in Wetherbury later, so we can keep our eyes open for fairy magic!"

After lunch the girls wrapped up warmly and set off into town, leaving Mr Tate struggling to fix the Christmas tree lights. Although the sun was shining in the pale blue sky, there was a frosty chill in the air.

"Maybe we'll have some snow tonight," Kirsty said eagerly.

"Look," Rachel said, nudging her friend. "The electricians are trying to fix the illuminations."

Two men on top of long ladders were busy tinkering with the bulbs, as shoppers milled around in the street below.

"They won't have much luck unless we get the magic candle back,"

Kirsty whispered.

The square was full of market stalls and busy shops. The floats and the platform from the previous evening were gone and a tall Christmas tree had been set up in their place. It was decorated with shiny baubles, tinsel and fairy lights, although the lights weren't working.

A small group of children were gathered on one side of the tree, holding candles in silver holders and singing carols.

"Doesn't that sound Christmassy?"
Kirsty said with a grin, as the girls
walked closer to the sound of the
children's voices.

"Yes, but I think someone's singing out
of tune!" Rachel whispered to Kirsty.

Kirsty nodded. She had noticed one
child who was a little
shorter than the
others. He was
muffled up in a
big coat with a
hood and a long
thick scarf, and he
was singing very
loudly but not very
well.

"It's the one in the big coat," she
whispered.

"He may not be able to sing very well," Rachel whispered back, "but he's got the best candle!"

Kirsty stared at the candle. It was bigger and rounder than the ones the other children were holding, and it was a very bright white which almost seemed to glow with hidden fire. Looking closely, Kirsty saw tiny white and silver sparkles swirl around the candle.

"Rachel, I think he's got the magic

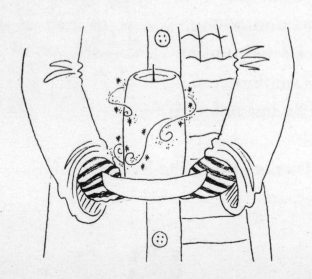

candle!" Kirsty gasped. "He must be a goblin!"

Her heart thumping with excitement, Rachel stared at the carol-singer. As he moved, she just caught a glimpse of a green nose poking over the top of his scarf.

"It is a goblin!" she said to Kirsty. "But how are we going to get the candle back?"

"Hello, Rachel!" a tiny voice sang out beside her.

Rachel jumped and turned to see Stella peeping out from behind a shiny bauble on the Christmas tree.

"I've spotted my magic candle too!" Stella whispered, as Rachel and Kirsty gathered round the bauble to hide her from view. "But I don't know how to get it back. Any ideas?"

Rachel and Kirsty fell silent for a moment, thinking. Then Kirsty's face broke into a smile. "I've thought of something that might work!" she said. "Stella, could you magic up a copy of the magic candle?"

"Yes, I think so," she replied. "But it won't be magical like the real candle."

"That doesn't matter," said Kirsty, "as long as it fools the goblin."

"I'll do my best," Stella promised. She frowned in concentration and waved her wand. Immediately, green sparkles whizzed and fizzed around in front of her, and the copycat candle started to take form.

Chapter Four
A Sweet Trick

The green sparkles faded away and a candle appeared in Kirsty's hand. It was a perfect copy of the magic candle – except that it was pink!

"Oh, dear!" Stella laughed. "Let's have another go."

She waved her wand again. This time,

as the sparkles died away, Rachel and
Kirsty watched the candle slowly turn
from pink to white.

"Perfect!" said Kirsty,
tucking the candle into
her pocket. "Now,
wait here."

Kirsty set off across
the square while
Rachel and Stella kept an eye on the
goblin. When she came back she was
carrying two paper bags.

"What are those?" Rachel asked curiously.

"Sweets," Kirsty replied, opening the bags. Rachel peeped in and saw stripy mint humbugs in one bag and fruit sweets in coloured wrappers in the other.

"Now, you take these, Rachel," Kirsty said, handing the humbugs to her friend as the carol-singers finished their song. "And go and offer all the carol-singers a sweetie!"

Looking a bit puzzled, Rachel did as she was told. "Merry Christmas!" she said, holding the bag out to the singers nearest her.

"Oh, thank you!" they replied, each

taking a sweet.

Kirsty watched the goblin as Rachel carried on handing out sweets. He was looking very eager as he waited his turn, but before Rachel reached him, Kirsty stepped forwards. "Here, have a sweet!" she said, holding out her bag.

Greedily the goblin thrust his gloved hand into the bag and pulled out a whole fistful of sweets. He didn't even say thank you. But then a look of dismay

 came over his face as he stared at the sweets in his hand. Kirsty grinned to herself. The goblin had just realised that

he couldn't unwrap his sweets and hold
the candle at the same time!

Rachel and Stella could now see what
Kirsty's clever plan was.

"What's the matter?" Kirsty asked the
goblin. "Don't you like sweets?"

"Yes, but I can't unwrap them while
I'm holding this candle!" the goblin
grumbled.

Kirsty held out her
hand. "Why don't you
let me hold it for you?"
she offered politely.

Rachel and Stella
exchanged a hopeful
look as they waited
for the goblin to reply.

"Oh, no!" the goblin
said quickly, his eyes

moving shiftily from side to side. "This is
a very special candle!"

"But I'll be standing right next to you
the whole time," Kirsty assured him.

The goblin still looked doubtful, so
Rachel decided to lend Kirsty a hand.
She took a sweet from Kirsty's bag and
unwrapped it right under the goblin's
nose. Then she popped it into her
mouth.

"Mmm!" she said. "These sweets

are really delicious!"

The goblin stared longingly at the sweets while Kirsty held her breath. Would he give in and let her take the candle, or not?

Chapter Five
Candlelight

After a moment, the goblin could stand it no longer. "Here!" he said gruffly, and he thrust the magic candle at Kirsty.

Kirsty took the candle and breathed a silent sigh of relief. Now that his hands were free, the goblin started unwrapping sweets as fast as he could. Then he crammed them into his mouth, all at the same time.

While the goblin was stuffing himself, Kirsty quietly pulled out the fake candle. Quickly she swapped it with the magic candle and slipped it into her pocket.

"I'll have that back now," the goblin mumbled through a mouthful of sweets. He snatched the candle rudely from Kirsty and turned his back on her.

Kirsty winked at
Rachel and they
moved over to the
Christmas tree
where Stella was
hidden.

"Well done,
girls!" the little
fairy whispered,
her eyes shining.
"You've got the
candle!"

"And the goblin hasn't even noticed!"
Kirsty laughed.

They all looked over at the goblin who
was happily trying to sing through a
mouthful of sweets.

"Let's take the candle back to
Fairyland where it belongs!" Stella

said. While everyone was watching the
carol-singers, she raised her wand and
showered Kirsty and Rachel with fairy
sparkles. The girls felt themselves shrinking
to fairy size as they were whisked away in
a swirl of magic dust.

A few moments later, the girls were
flying over Fairyland with glittering,
gauzy wings on their backs. Below,
they could see red and white toadstool
houses, and the fairy palace with a huge
Christmas tree standing in front of it.

As Stella and the girls fluttered down towards the ground, they saw the King and Queen waiting to greet them.

"We have the magic candle!" Stella announced.

"Kirsty and Rachel, welcome to Fairyland once more!" said King Oberon.

"And you have found our magic candle," Queen Titania added happily. "We cannot thank you and Stella enough."

"We're glad to help," Kirsty said, and

Rachel nodded.

Stella turned towards them. "Girls, would you like to put the candle back on the tree?" she asked.

Both girls nodded and Kirsty took the candle from her pocket. The branches of the tree were decorated with candles in silver holders, but the biggest and most beautiful holder was empty.

As Rachel held the branch steady, Kirsty carefully slotted the candle into place. Immediately, it began to glow, giving off magical, fiery sparks.

"We'll do our best to find the bauble and the star, too,"

Rachel promised the King and Queen.

"Thank you," said Queen Titania with a smile. "And now you must return to Wetherbury and see how beautiful it looks, thanks to you two bringing the magic candle home!"

She lifted her wand and Rachel and Kirsty just had time to wave goodbye to Stella, before they were whisked away in a swirl of silver sparkles.

A moment later, the girls found themselves back in Wetherbury square.

Nobody seemed to have noticed that they'd vanished and reappeared again.

Everyone was too busy staring up at the Christmas illuminations, which were now working perfectly.

"Look, the goblin still hasn't realised he's been tricked!" whispered Kirsty.

The girls glanced at the goblin who was singing away happily, then joined the crowd of shoppers admiring the illuminations. Every single bulb was now alight, and the glittering snowflakes stood out brilliantly against the black velvet of the night sky.

Kirsty beamed at Rachel.

"Aren't they beautiful?"
Rachel nodded.
"We've made a good
start," she said. "Now
we've got to find the
bauble and the star."

"Yes," Kirsty agreed
with a smile. "But
right now we'd better get on with our
Christmas shopping, or our friends and
families won't get any presents this year!"

"You're right!" Rachel laughed, and
the two girls headed for the shops, the
illuminations shining brightly overhead.

Story Two
Snowballs and Baubles

Chapter Six
A Snowy Start

"Kirsty! Wake up!"

Kirsty rolled over in bed. "What's the matter, Rachel?" she asked sleepily.

Rachel, who was at the window in her pyjamas, grinned at her. "It's snowing!"

"Really?" Fully awake now, Kirsty bounced out of bed and rushed over to the window. She peered out. Great white flakes of snow were drifting down from the grey sky.

"I hope it snows for ages," Rachel said eagerly. "It would be brilliant to have a white Christmas."

"Look, it's falling faster and faster," Kirsty pointed out.

The girls stood at the window, watching the snowflakes swirl, before they got dressed. The snow began to settle thickly on the lawn and flowerbeds in the garden, and showed no signs of stopping.

"If we get a lot of snow, we could go to the park after lunch and build a snowman," Kirsty suggested, as she brushed her hair.

"Ooh, that sounds great!" exclaimed Rachel. She was so excited, she almost lost her balance as she pulled on her jeans.

The girls went downstairs. In the
lounge, Kirsty's dad was on his hands
and knees tinkering with the Christmas
tree lights. Mrs Tate
was helping him.

"Morning, girls,"
she said with a smile.

Mr Tate scratched
his head. "I don't
understand it," he
muttered, looking
puzzled.

"We've checked the wiring and the
fuse is fine, but these fairy lights still
won't come on."

"Why don't you leave them now
and have some breakfast?" suggested
Kirsty's mum.

"Not yet," Mr Tate replied, frowning. "I

think I've almost got it . . . "

Smiling, Mrs Tate shook her head and went off to the kitchen. Rachel and Kirsty followed.

"The lights won't come back on until the magic bauble has been returned to Fairyland," Kirsty whispered to Rachel. "Maybe we'll find it today."

After breakfast, the girls spent the morning wrapping Christmas presents. But they kept an eye on the weather. To their delight, the snow fell heavily all morning, and by lunchtime the back garden was covered in a thick white blanket.

After lunch, the

girls slipped on
their coats and
boots.

"Mum, can
Rachel and I
go to the park?"
Kirsty asked.

Mrs Tate nodded.
"Make sure you're home in time for tea.
Hopefully the fairy lights will be fixed by
then," she added with a smile, "otherwise
I'll have to start serving your dad his
meals under the tree!"

Rachel and Kirsty laughed, and rushed
out of the back door.

They set off, stomping through the
snow in their wellies, and by the time
they got to the park their cheeks were
pink and glowing.

The park was full of people. Some were building snowmen, others were sledging and having snowball fights. But Rachel and Kirsty quickly found a quiet spot, not far from a group of six children who were building a snowman.

"Let's make the body first," Kirsty suggested, rolling a snowball in her mittened hands. She put it on the snowy

ground and she and Rachel began to roll
it around so it got bigger and bigger. Then
they made a smaller one for the head.

"See if you can find some pebbles,
Rachel," Kirsty panted, as she lifted the
snowman's head on to the top of his body.

Rachel rooted around in a flowerbed
and managed to find a small handful of
pebbles. She and Kirsty pressed the

pebbles into the snowman, giving him
eyes, a smiley mouth and four buttons
down his chest.

"Isn't he handsome?" Kirsty said with a
grin.

"Not without a nose!" laughed Rachel.
"I'll look for a twig or something."

"Will this do?" called a silvery voice.

The girls spun round and stared up at

the sky. Stella the Star Fairy was flying
towards them, clutching a long thin
carrot in her arms.

"Perfect!" Kirsty agreed, as Stella
landed on the snowman's head. She took
the carrot from the fairy and stuck it in
the middle of the snowman's face.

"What are you doing here, Stella?"
asked Rachel.

"Do you think the bauble might be nearby?" added Kirsty eagerly.

Stella nodded and flew over to sit on Rachel's shoulder. "Look over there," she whispered, pointing to the group of children nearby. "And take a good look at that snowman!"

Chapter Seven
A Very Suspicious Snowman

Wondering what Stella meant, Rachel and Kirsty glanced over at the group of children, who had finished their snowman and were now having a snowball fight. The girls edged closer to the other snowman, staring at it curiously.

It wasn't like any snowman they'd seen

before. For a start, it looked very mean. It had a big nose made of a large, pointed stone, a grinning mouth of black pebbles and enormous feet of snow.

"It looks a bit like a snow goblin!" Kirsty said slowly. Then she gasped and pointed at the children. "And if that's a snow goblin, who are they?"

"Maybe they're Jack Frost's goblins in disguise!" Rachel whispered.

"Exactly!" Stella replied. "In which case, they might have the bauble."

"I think we need to take a closer look," Kirsty said firmly.

Trying to keep out of sight, the girls made their way around the flowerbed and closer to the snowman. None of the children noticed them. They were too busy hurling snowballs at each other.

The girls peered at them, but they were so muffled up in hoods, scarves and coats that it was hard to tell if they were goblins or not.

As the girls watched, one of the
children was hit in the face by a large
snowball. With a screech of rage, he tore
his wet scarf away, revealing a mean,
green, warty face!

"They are goblins!" Kirsty exclaimed.

"I'll get you for that!" the goblin
yelled, shaking the snow from his big
nose and stamping his foot. "I'm going
to shove a snowball down the back of

your neck!"

"You'll have
to catch me
first!" the
goblin who
had thrown the
snowball jeered.
He kicked lumps

of snow at the other goblin, then ran
away to hide behind a tree, laughing his
head off.

"The bauble might be around here
somewhere," Rachel said hopefully.
"Maybe we should look for it."

"We'll have to get a bit closer," Kirsty
said, creeping forwards.

"Please be careful, girls," Stella
whispered anxiously.

Rachel and Kirsty began to edge

towards the goblins, with Stella sitting on
Rachel's shoulder and peeping out from
under her hood. Snowballs were flying
everywhere. As Kirsty, Rachel and Stella
watched, a goblin wearing a red scarf
threw a snowball so hard that he slipped
and fell on his face.

"Ha ha ha!" the other goblins roared
with delight.

Moaning and grumbling, the goblin scrambled to his feet. "Stop laughing at me!" he spluttered through a mouthful of snow. Then, as one of the laughing goblins bent to make another snowball, the goblin with the red scarf rushed over and shoved a snowball down the back of his blue coat.

"Arggh!" yelled the goblin in the blue

coat angrily. "That's cold!"

"They're so covered in snow, they look like snow goblins themselves now!" Kirsty muttered, trying not to laugh.

Rachel giggled, then covered her mouth with her hand; she didn't want the goblins to notice her.

Suddenly Kirsty frowned. "What's that goblin doing over there?" she whispered.

Until now, neither Stella nor the girls had noticed that one goblin was sitting on the ground, cross-legged, rolling snowballs. He had obviously decided that the best way to win the fight was to gather lots of snowballs in advance, and there was already a large pile of them beside him. As he carefully rolled another, a goblin in a woolly hat dashed over and tried to take the snowball from the top of the heap.

Looking furious, the sitting goblin dropped the snowball he was holding, and slapped the other's hand. "Make your own snowballs!" he shouted angrily, and tidied up his snowball pile.

Kirsty looked at him a little more closely, and then nudged Rachel. "Look," she hissed.

Rachel looked and saw that in the goblin's lap was something round and sparkling, but it wasn't a snowball. It was pure white, even whiter than the snow, and it flashed and glittered

in the sunlight with every colour of
the rainbow.

"It's the magic bauble!" Stella
whispered in delight.

Chapter Eight
Girls Under Fire

"It's beautiful!" Rachel sighed. "We must get it back."

"But how?" Kirsty murmured thoughtfully.

The girls and Stella watched the goblins, wondering how they could get hold of the bauble. The sitting goblin

was much more interested in snowballs
than the bauble, but he kept glancing
up suspiciously to check that none of
his companions was trying to steal from
his snowball heap. That made it very
difficult for the girls to get close to him
without being seen.

Meanwhile the snowball fight was

getting fiercer. The
goblin in the blue
coat had hurried off
to hide behind a tree
and shake the snow
out of his clothes. But
the one in the red
scarf sneaked around
the other side of the
tree, threw an armful
of snow over his rival

and then ran off to hide behind two other goblins.

Yelling with rage, the goblin in the blue coat gave chase and flung a big snowball at his enemy. Unfortunately, it hit the two other goblins and they shrieked with fury.

Now nearly all the goblins were covered in snow and ready to do battle.

They started taking sides – the goblin in the red scarf and his two friends against the goblin in the blue coat and the one in the woolly hat.

"Hey!" the goblin in the red scarf shouted to the sitting goblin, as he and his teammate were pelted heavily with snowballs. "Come and help us! It's two against three here!"

The sitting
goblin grinned
and jumped
to his feet, not
realising that
as he did so,
the gleaming
magic bauble
fell off his lap
and landed

softly on the snowy ground.
He quickly scooped up his snowballs and
ran to join the fight.

Rachel and Kirsty glanced at each
other.

"Let's try and grab the bauble!" Rachel
whispered.

Kirsty nodded.

As the shrieking goblins hurled

snowballs at each other, Kirsty and
Rachel began to edge their way towards
the bauble. It lay there, sparkling prettily,
but just as Kirsty was about to stretch
out her hand and pick it up, a large
snowball suddenly hit
her on the shoulder.

"Stop them!"
shouted a gruff goblin
voice.

The girls had been
spotted and, to their
dismay, all six goblins
were now running in their direction,
flinging snowballs at them.

"Quick!" Rachel gasped, as one hit her
on the arm. "Behind that tree!"

Forced to leave the bauble where it
was, Rachel and Kirsty dashed behind

the tree as a huge shower of snowballs
followed them.

"How are we going to get the bauble
back now?" Rachel panted. "We can't
get past six goblins!"

"Wait!" Stella said suddenly. She flew
up to a branch of the tree, her eyes

shining. "I'll turn you girls into fairies,
and then we'll all be small enough
to dodge the snowballs!" she declared
happily.

"But if the goblins are throwing
snowballs at us, that means they know
we're there," Kirsty pointed out. "And we
don't want them to see us."

"Oh, yes, we do!" laughed Stella. "We
want the goblins to see us and pelt us

with snowballs!"

Kirsty and Rachel stared at Stella
in amazement.

"How will it help to have lots of
snowballs thrown at us?" asked Rachel.

"Trust me!" Stella told her with a
cheeky grin. "My plan is going to work.
I'm sure of it!"

Chapter Nine
A Daring Plan

Rachel and Kirsty had no idea what
Stella was up to, but they glanced at
each other and grinned. They both
loved being fairy-sized, so they waited
eagerly while Stella waved her wand and
scattered magic fairy dust over them. A
moment later they had shrunk to the

same size as their fairy friend and fairy
wings shimmered on their backs.

"Here we go!" Stella said,
fluttering out from behind
the tree. "Now make lots
of noise, girls, and make
sure the goblins see us!"

Still feeling puzzled,
Kirsty and Rachel zoomed
up into the air behind Stella
and headed towards the goblins.

"Yoohoo!" Rachel called,
waving her arms.

"Over here!" yelled Kirsty.

While Stella and the girls
had been behind the tree, the
goblins had clearly been stockpiling
snowballs. Now they looked up, and
their warty faces darkened with rage.

"Here come those pesky fairies!" one goblin shouted.

"Get them!" snarled another. All the goblins began hurling snowballs at Rachel, Kirsty and Stella.

"This is scary!" Kirsty panted as a large snowball whistled past her ear. Now that she was so tiny, the snowballs seemed as big as houses.

"Well done, girls!" Stella called, as Rachel fluttered out of the way of another snowball. "Now, watch!"

As yet another snowball whizzed past Stella,

she lifted her wand and sprinkled magic fairy dust over it. Rachel and Kirsty watched curiously as the snowball changed in mid-air to become an exact copy of the magic bauble.

"Look!" shouted the goblin in the blue coat furiously. "One of you just threw the bauble instead of a snowball! What an idiot!"

"Who're you calling an idiot?" yelled the goblin with the woolly hat, beginning to throw snowballs at him instead of at Stella and the girls.

"Stop it!" the first goblin panted, dodging out of the way, "We have to get the bauble back!"

Arguing and grumbling, the six goblins dashed after the fake bauble, which had fallen to the ground just below Rachel, Stella and Kirsty.

"Keep those fairies away from the bauble!" shouted one of the goblins and, as they ran, the goblins all began hurling snowballs at Stella, Rachel and Kirsty.

"Can you see the real bauble, girls?" called Stella.

Rachel and Kirsty peered through the hail of snowballs. The bauble had rolled to a stop near the edge of the flowerbed.

"I see it!" Rachel shouted.

"Good," Stella replied, raising her wand again. "You go and get it while I give the goblins something else to chase!"

She waved her wand and suddenly the
air was full of magic sparkles.
This time, to Kirsty
and Rachel's
amazement, all
the snowballs flying
through the air
turned into fake
baubles.

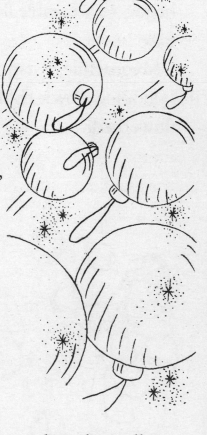

"What's going on?"
yelled the goblin in
the red scarf, hardly
able to believe his
eyes. He skidded to
a halt as the baubles
began to fall to the
ground around him,
and the other goblins
banged right into him so that they all

ended up in a snowy heap.

"Pesky fairies! Which is the real bauble?" one goblin spluttered as they all began to scramble around picking up the fake ones.

Meanwhile, Kirsty and Rachel were swooping down to the edge of the flowerbed.

"We'll both have to lift the bauble now that we're fairy-sized," Kirsty panted as she landed on the ground. "And we'll have to do it quickly, before the goblins see what we're up to!"

Chapter Ten
Up, Up and Away!

Rachel and Kirsty both took hold of the bauble.

"Now!" Rachel whispered.

Both girls fluttered their wings, struggling to fly upwards while lifting the bauble. To their relief, it was just light enough for them to carry. Gradually the girls rose into the air, higher and higher, until they were out of the goblins' reach.

As Rachel and Kirsty hovered in mid-air, holding the sparkling bauble, they saw the goblins down below. They had given up searching, and had started arguing instead.

"Who was the idiot that threw the

bauble in the first place?" one of them grumbled.

"Well, it wasn't ME!" another goblin retorted.

"I bet it's YOUR fault!" the first goblin shouted, prodding another in the stomach.

"No, it's HIS fault!" the prodded goblin snapped, pushing the goblin in the woolly hat over. With a howl of rage, the woolly-hatted goblin tumbled backwards into a deep snowdrift and disappeared from view.

Immediately, the other goblins began pushing and shoving each other until they all ended up stuck in the snowdrift, their arms and legs waving frantically.

Meanwhile, a beaming Stella flew over to join Rachel and Kirsty. "We did it, girls!" Stella beamed, her eyes shining. "And now I think it's time we took the magic bauble straight back to Fairyland."

She lifted her wand and in a whirl of green sparkles, Rachel and Kirsty were whisked away, the goblins' grumbles

ringing in their
ears.

As they flew
over Fairyland,
Rachel and Kirsty
looked down to
see a large crowd
of fairies waiting around
the Christmas tree by
the royal palace.
Everyone looked very
anxious, but when they saw Stella,
Rachel and Kirsty flying towards them
with the magic bauble, they clapped
their hands in joy.

"Thank you, thank you," cried Queen
Titania, coming to greet the girls as they
landed.

"Our precious bauble is safely home

again," King Oberon declared, smiling.

"Rachel, Kirsty, would you put the
bauble back on the tree for us?" Stella
asked sweetly.

"We'd love to!" Rachel and Kirsty
chorused, and they carried the bauble
over to the tree.

There were baubles on every branch,
except for a big one near the middle.
Carefully the girls hung the bauble on
the branch, where it swayed gently,
glittering and gleaming and
sending flashes
of rainbow
colours here
and there.

"We left the
goblins stuck
in a snowdrift!"
Stella told the King
and Queen with a grin.

"They were arguing so much, it'll take
them ages to dig themselves out!" Kirsty
added.

Everyone laughed, but then Queen
Titania sighed.

"Stella, Rachel and Kirsty," she said solemnly, "you have done very well to return the candle and the bauble. But the

last decoration, the star, is the most important of all!"

"Why?" Rachel asked.

"Because without the magic star, the stars will not twinkle in the night sky," the Queen explained. "And without the stars, Father Christmas can't find his way to deliver the presents on Christmas Eve."

"You mean nobody will get any presents?" gasped Kirsty.

The Queen nodded.

"And Christmas Eve is tomorrow," Rachel said. "We don't have much time left!"

"At least we know where the star is," Stella pointed out. "It's hidden somewhere in Goblin Grotto."

"Then we'll have to go there and get it back!" Kirsty said in a determined voice. "Can you take us Stella?"

The little fairy nodded solemnly.

"We won't let you down," Rachel told the King and Queen firmly.

"Thank you," Queen Titania replied. "And now I think you both deserve a good rest. Go home, and forget all about the goblins until tomorrow."

The two girls said their goodbyes as the Fairy Queen waved her wand. In a swirl of fairy dust, the girls were swept up and carried home. They landed gently on Kirsty's front doorstep.

"We must find the star tomorrow, Kirsty," Rachel sighed.

"Yes," Kirsty agreed. "Christmas just won't be Christmas without Santa."

Suddenly, Rachel pointed at the window of the lounge. "Look, Kirsty!" she said, smiling all over her face. "Your Christmas tree fairy lights are working again!"

"Hurrah!" Kirsty cried happily.

The two girls rushed inside.

Mr Tate was sitting on the sofa, looking very pleased with himself. "Well, I fixed the lights, girls," he announced. "It was just a matter of changing every bulb on the string."

Rachel and Kirsty smiled at each other.

"That's what Dad thinks," Kirsty whispered.

"But we know better!" Rachel added.

Story Three
Search for the Star

Chapter Eleven
Girls Become Goblins!

"I wonder what Goblin Grotto is like," Rachel said, excitedly. It was Christmas Eve, and she and Kirsty were out in the Tate's back garden, sweeping the snow off the paths. "Do you think it'll be scary?"

"I hope not!" Kirsty replied with a

laugh, brushing away the last heap of
snow.

"But don't forget, we'll have Stella
there with all her lovely fairy magic to
help us!"

Rachel grinned and nodded. "But how
will we get the star without the goblins
seeing us?" she went on. "I mean, even
if we're fairy-sized, there's still a chance
we'll be spotted."

"I know," Kirsty agreed. "But it's not going to stop us from trying, is it?"

"Of course not!" Rachel said in a determined voice. "We have to get the star back or there will be no real stars in the night sky to guide Santa when he's delivering presents!"

Rachel shaded her eyes and gazed across the garden. "Kirsty, look at that cute little robin."

Kirsty looked where Rachel was pointing. A robin was bobbing through the air, coming straight towards them.

"There's something on its back," Kirsty

said in surprise.

"Hello, girls!" called a tiny, silvery voice.

"It's Stella!" Rachel gasped.

The fairy was riding along on the robin's back, waving at Rachel and Kirsty. The little bird landed on the fence, and Stella hopped off. She patted the robin's head, and it flew away into a nearby tree.

"Are you here to take us to Goblin Grotto?" asked Rachel.

Stella nodded. "Are you sure you want to do this, girls?" she asked, her face very serious.

"Of course we do!" Rachel replied firmly.

"But we're a bit worried about getting spotted by the goblins," Kirsty added. "We need some sort of disguise."

"Oh!" Rachel exclaimed suddenly. "Maybe we could disguise ourselves as goblins!"

"That's a great idea!" Kirsty agreed eagerly. "Could you make us goblin-sized and green, Stella?"

"Oh, yes!" the fairy laughed. "Then if

we wrap our scarves around our faces
and put up our hoods like the goblins
have been doing, no one will notice us!"
Rachel declared happily.

"Here goes, then," Stella cried, and
she waved her wand, sending sparkling
fairy dust spinning all around the girls.
Immediately they shrank down to the
size of goblins.

"Am I
green?" asked
Kirsty. Then she
caught sight of
Rachel's face
and burst out
laughing. Her
friend was as
green as the
greenest goblin!

Rachel was
laughing too hard
at Kirsty's emerald-
coloured face to
answer.

"You're both green
all over!" Stella
said with a smile, as the girls took off
their gloves and laughed again at their
green fingers. "There's just one problem
though," she went on with a frown. "My
magic can't make you look mean and
nasty like the goblins. So you'll have to
do that yourselves."

Kirsty and Rachel were still giggling at
each other's strangely coloured faces.

"Try to look as angry and grumpy as
you can," Stella told them.

Rachel and Kirsty managed to stop

laughing, and Rachel screwed up her face into a frown, while Kirsty scowled and narrowed her eyes.

"Not mean and nasty enough," Stella declared. "Try again."

This time both girls hunched their shoulders and screwed up their faces into the ugliest, grumpiest frowns they could manage.

"Well, you don't look quite as nasty as real goblins," Stella laughed, "but it'll

have to do!"

"Let's wrap ourselves up well, Rachel," Kirsty said. "That will help to hide our faces."

Quickly the girls wound their scarves around the lower part of their faces and pulled up their hoods.

"Now," Stella went on, "are you ready to come with me to Goblin Grotto, my goblin friends?"

Both girls nodded eagerly, and with a flick of Stella's wand and a shower of magic sparkles, they were on their way!

Chapter Twelve
Starshine in Goblin Grotto

Seconds later, in a whirl of fairy magic, Stella, Rachel and Kirsty arrived at Goblin Grotto. The two girls had never been there before, and they stared around curiously.

The goblins lived in small wooden huts which were dotted here and there

around the foot of a snow-covered hill.
Smoke curled from the chimneys of all
the houses. The ground was covered with
thick snow and ice, and the sky overhead
was grim and grey with no sign of the
sun. In the distance, at the top of the hill,
Rachel and Kirsty could see Jack Frost's
Ice Castle. A cold, grey mist drifted
around its frozen blue turrets.

"*Brr,*" whispered
Kirsty, wrapping her
arms round herself. "It's
even colder here than it
is at home!"

Rachel, who was
closest to one of the
wooden huts, peered
cautiously through the

window. A fire was burning merrily in
the hearth, and a goblin was slumped
in an armchair in front of it. He was
stretching out his toes to the flames, and
mumbling under his breath.

"Oh, my feet are frozen!" he
complained.

Rachel smiled. "Look," she whispered
to Kirsty. "I'd forgotten how much
goblins hate to have cold feet."

Kirsty peeped through the window and grinned.

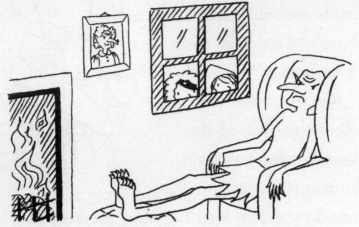

"Girls!" Stella gasped, tapping Rachel on the shoulder. "Someone's coming!"

Suddenly feeling very scared, Rachel and Kirsty spun round. A big goblin with a wart on the end of his nose was tramping down the snowy track towards them.

"Quick, Stella!" Kirsty said urgently. "Hide!"

"All right," Stella whispered. "But put on your grumpiest faces, girls."

The fairy fluttered out of sight behind the wooden hut, and Kirsty and Rachel screwed their faces up into ugly frowns. Hearts thumping madly, they waited as the goblin came closer. Would he realise that they were humans in disguise, and not goblins at all?

As the goblin passed by, he threw the two girls a grumpy look. "What are you staring at?" he snapped.

Rachel and Kirsty didn't reply, and the

goblin trudged on his way. Both girls sighed with relief.

"Our disguise worked!" Kirsty breathed.

"Well done, girls," Stella said, flying out from behind the hut. "Now we must find the star!"

Rachel's face fell. "But how are we going to find it?" she asked. "We can't search the houses if there are goblins inside them."

Kirsty nodded thoughtfully and gazed around. Suddenly her eyes opened wide. "Actually, I don't think finding the star is going to be a problem," she said. "But getting it down might be!"

Rachel and Stella looked puzzled.

"What do you mean, Kirsty?" asked Rachel.

"Look," Kirsty replied, pointing down the track.

Stella and Rachel turned to see what Kirsty was pointing at.

There, in the middle of the goblin village, above the roofs of the wooden huts, they could just see the tip of a tall Christmas tree. Perched on the very top was a large, silver star. It shimmered and shone in the cold, grey air. And as it sparkled, every so often it sent dazzling darts of silver fairy dust shooting into the sky.

"It's the star from the Fairyland Christmas tree!" Stella exclaimed in delight. "You've found it!"

Chapter Thirteen
Catch a Falling Star

Rachel, Kirsty and Stella stared up at the star.

"Quick, let's go and get it right away!" Stella whispered urgently.

As fast as they could, the girls hurried after Stella along the snow-covered track to the centre of the village.

"How will we get the star down?" asked Kirsty anxiously.

"Without all those goblins seeing us!" Rachel added, stopping dead as she stared at the scene ahead of her.

A crowd of grown-up goblins and goblin children were gathered near the Christmas tree, having a party. They were all wrapped up warmly in hats, scarves and coats. One was selling hot pies, and there was a group of carol-

GOBLIN GRUB

singers holding lanterns.
They were all singing
out of tune, just like the
goblin who'd had the
magic candle. They
sounded so bad that
Kirsty wanted to
put her hands
over her ears!
"Goblins
aren't very good
singers, are they?"
she whispered to
Rachel.

Rachel shook her
head. "But they seem to
be enjoying themselves," she
whispered back, as the goblins
launched into another tuneless song.

"We have to get the star down somehow," Stella said thoughtfully. "Girls, if I try to fly up and push the star off the top of the tree without being spotted, will you try to catch it?"

"Yes, that's a great idea," Rachel said with a grin.

"We'll go and stand under the tree, as close as we can get," Kirsty whispered to Stella. "Good luck!"

Stella zoomed off, and Rachel turned to Kirsty.

"Let's join the party," she said.
"But we'd better try and sing out of
tune, or they might guess we're not real
goblins!"

Putting on their
nastiest faces,
Rachel and Kirsty
hurried over to join
the carol-singers.
None of the
goblins gave them
a second glance
as they stood at

the back of the group. Then the girls began
to sing, doing their best to sound flat and
tuneless as they inched closer to the tree.

"There's Stella!" Kirsty whispered to
Rachel under cover of the loud noise.

Rachel glanced upwards. Stella was flying

high overhead, taking cover behind the grey clouds. She hovered above the tree, looking nervously this way and that, and then began to float downwards.

Suddenly the goblin standing next to  Kirsty elbowed her in the ribs. Kirsty almost fell over with fright. Had he noticed Stella?

"You're singing out of tune!"he said with a scowl.

"Sorry!" Kirsty muttered, as gruffly as she could. She decided to sing more quietly.

Rachel could see that Stella had landed on the top of the tree, and was now releasing the star from the cords which

held it. When she
was ready, the little
fairy waved at
Rachel. Carefully,
Rachel edged right
up to the tree. Then,
as Stella pushed the
star gently off the
top, Rachel held out
her hands.

The star fell
towards her,
sparkling as
it tumbled
through the
air. It seemed
very bright to
Rachel and she
was sure one of the

goblins would spot it, but to her relief, nobody seemed to notice and she caught it safely before it hit the ground. Quickly she pushed it out of sight beneath her

coat, and edged her way back to Kirsty.

"I've got it!" she whispered joyfully.

"Great!" Kirsty beamed.

"What are you whispering about?"

snapped the grumpy goblin next to her. He stared curiously at the girls and they both began to feel quite nervous.

"Do your best grumpy face," Rachel muttered. She and Kirsty pulled their faces into angry frowns, but the goblin didn't stop staring.

"Look!" one of the other carol-singers shouted suddenly. "The star is missing from the top of the Christmas tree!"

All the goblins looked up at this, and began to mutter angrily as they saw that the star had gone.

"Where is it?"

"Did it fall off?"

"Who's taken it?"

Then there was another shout from the goblin selling pies. "Look up there!" he cried, pointing towards the top of the tree. "Is that a fairy?"

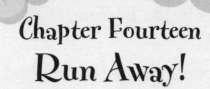

Chapter Fourteen
Run Away!

Rachel and Kirsty stared at each other in horror, then glanced up at Stella. The tiny fairy must have heard the goblin's shout, for she darted quickly out of sight behind one of the large glass baubles hanging on the tree.

Rachel looked down at the front of

her coat. To her dismay, she saw that magical, silvery sparks were shooting out from between the buttons. "Oh, no!" she whispered.

The goblin next to Rachel had noticed the sparks too. He was staring at them, looking puzzled. He peered at Rachel's face, and suddenly his face broke into a frown. "You're not a goblin!" he hissed, stepping in front of her. "You've stolen our star!"

Right at that moment, Kirsty, who was still staring upwards at the tree, suddenly felt her hood slip backwards.

"A girl!" yelled the goblin standing next to her. He was staring at Kirsty as if his eyes were going to pop out. "A human girl!"

"And they've got the star!" screeched the one who had spotted Rachel.

Rachel pushed past him and grabbed Kirsty's hand. "RUN!" she yelled.

The two girls broke away from
the crowd of goblins, but the goblins
immediately gave chase, shouting loudly
and pushing each other out of the way.
Kirsty looked back at the tree anxiously,
and saw Stella zooming after them.

"Which way?" Rachel panted, as they
came to a fork in the track.

"This way!" Kirsty took off down the left-hand fork, and Rachel followed. She took a quick glance over her shoulder, and her heart sank. Other goblins were coming out of their houses to see what the noise was about, and they were joining in the chase. Now there were about fifty goblins running after the girls!

"What's going on?" shouted a gruff
voice ahead of them. Rachel and
Kirsty saw the goblin who had been
toasting his toes by the fire, standing in
the middle of the track. Like the other
goblins, he had heard the noise and
come to see what was going on.

"Stop them!" shouted the goblins

behind the girls.
"They've stolen the
magic star!"
The goblin looked
very grave and held
up his hand.
"STOP!" he roared.
But Rachel and
Kirsty didn't stop.

They dashed past the goblin, one on
each side. The goblin was spun round like

a spinning-
top, and
landed on his
back in the
snow.

"Oh!"
he howled.
"I'm frozen!"

"Come on, girls!" Stella urged. She had
caught up with Rachel and Kirsty, and
now she hovered over their heads as they
ran down yet another track.

Kirsty was racking her brains, trying to think of an escape plan. If Stella turns us into fairies, we can fly away, she thought, but then she realised that that wouldn't work. The star was too big for a fairy to carry, and they couldn't leave it behind.

Suddenly, she realised that they were running back into the middle of the village. Both girls slid to a halt by the Christmas tree.

"We've run around in a great big circle!" Rachel groaned in dismay.

"And here come the goblins!" Kirsty panted, her face very pale.

The goblins were rushing towards them from all directions.

"Now we've got you!" one yelled, and the others cheered.

Kirsty turned to Stella. "Stella, if Rachel and I were fairy-sized, do you think the three of us could carry the star between us?" she asked urgently. "Each of us could hold a corner of it."

"I don't know," Stella replied doubtfully.
"It's quite heavy."

"We'll have to try!" Rachel gasped,
laying the star carefully on the ground.
"It's our only chance!"

As the goblins surrounded them, Stella
raised her wand.

"There's the star!" one of the goblins
shouted.
"Grab it!"

But before the
goblins could
move, Stella's
magic fairy
dust drifted
over Rachel
and Kirsty.
Immediately

the goblin green faded away and the girls shrank to fairy-size. Both girls couldn't help shivering with fright as they gazed round at the angry goblins. They looked much bigger and scarier from a fairy's point of view!

"Quick!" Kirsty shouted, as the circle of goblins began to close in on them. "Grab a corner each and fly upwards as fast as you can!"

Chapter Fifteen
Flight to Fairyland

A moment later, Rachel, Kirsty and Stella shot upwards into the sky, lifting the star with them.

"We've done it!" Rachel cried joyfully.

The goblins below couldn't believe their eyes. They were so surprised, they couldn't stop themselves from colliding with the Christmas tree, and each other, as they rushed forwards. They all bumped their knobbly knees and long noses and fell in a tangled heap on the ground, groaning loudly.

"Watch out for the Christmas tree!" one of them shouted warningly.

Hovering high above the ground, Stella, Rachel and Kirsty watched as the huge Christmas tree tottered and swayed from side to side.

Slowly, it overbalanced and toppled over.

There were loud shrieks of rage as some of the big goblins were covered with tree branches, tinsel and other decorations, while a group of goblin children who were watching laughed so hard that they fell over too!

Stella turned to Rachel and Kirsty, a big smile across her face. "Let's get back to Fairyland right away!" she said. "It's almost night-time, and Father Christmas will want to start delivering his presents!"

Carrying the star, Stella, Rachel and
Kirsty flew to Fairyland as fast as their
wings could take them. When they
arrived, they found every single fairy in
the land waiting for them around the
Christmas tree, along with King Oberon
and Queen Titania. All the fairies gasped
with delight as they saw Stella and the
girls flying towards them with the magic
star.

"The star!" the fairies shouted

excitedly. "Christmas is saved!"

"You are just in time," King Oberon declared, beaming at Stella, Rachel and Kirsty as they flew down to the ground, clutching the star. "Father Christmas is about to set off on his delivery round!"

"Thank you so much," added Queen Titania gratefully. "Now, would you put the star back on the tree where it belongs?"

Stella, Rachel and Kirsty flew to the top of the tree and carefully lowered the star into

place. The star immediately shot dazzling swirls of magic silver fairy dust from every point, as if it knew it was home again.

"Girls, we all thank you from the

bottom of our hearts!" the King declared, as Rachel and Kirsty flew down to stand before him. "We can never repay you fully for your great kindness, but we can promise you an extra special Christmas!"

All of the fairies laughed and clapped,

and Kirsty and Rachel looked at each
other in delight.

"Thank you for your help, girls," Stella
said, kissing
them both
lightly on the
cheek. "And
I hope you
get everything
you want for
Christmas!"

"Now, we
mustn't keep you
any longer," the Queen
added. "You have to be home in time to
enjoy your own Christmas, after working
so hard."

"Merry Christmas, everybody!" Kirsty
and Rachel called, as Stella lifted her

wand to send them home.

"Merry Christmas!" the fairies
replied. They all waved their wands in
farewell, as Kirsty and Rachel were
swept gently off their feet in a whirl of
sparkling magic.

As the mist of fairy dust faded away, the
girls found themselves back in Kirsty's
back garden. It was getting dark, and the
lights were on in the Tate's house.

"Look!" Rachel pointed up at the night sky. "The stars are out."

Kirsty glanced upwards and saw with delight that the stars were twinkling brightly like tiny diamonds. "What's that over there?" she asked Rachel, pointing at a large shape moving swiftly across the sky.

Rachel screwed up her eyes as she tried

to make out what the shape might be. "It looks like a sleigh," she said slowly.

Kirsty's eyes opened wide. "It's Father Christmas!" she gasped.

The two girls watched in wonder as Father Christmas's sleigh, pulled by his magic reindeer, zoomed across the sky leaving a trail of golden sparks.

"Oh!" Kirsty cried suddenly. "The golden trail behind the sleigh is spelling out a message!"

Rachel caught her breath, her heart

pounding with excitement. She and Kirsty
stared up at the dark night sky, and there
against the inky blackness, they could
clearly read the words 'Merry Christmas,
Rachel and Kirsty!' written in dazzling
golden sparks.

As he passed over the Tate's garden,
Father Christmas looked down and
gave the girls a friendly wave, beaming
cheerfully at them. Then the sleigh picked
up speed and disappeared behind a cloud.
"He waved at us!" Kirsty laughed. "What

a lovely surprise!"

"That was wonderful!" Rachel agreed,
her eyes shining as she watched the fiery
golden letters fade away.

"Girls!" Mrs Tate called from inside
the house. "Rachel's parents are here to
collect her."

"I think it's going to be a very happy
Christmas, Rachel," Kirsty said with
a grin, as she and Rachel ran towards
the house.

"Yes. Merry Christmas, Kirsty!" laughed Rachel. "And a merry Christmas to everyone in Fairyland!"

The End

Have you met all the Christmas Fairies?

Now it's time for Kirsty and Rachel to help ...

Konnie the Christmas Cracker Fairy

Read on for a sneak peek ...

"This is going to be great," said Kirsty Tate, smiling at her best friend, Rachel Walker, as they arrived at the Tippington Community Centre.

It was almost Christmas, and Kirsty was staying with Rachel for the weekend. They had tied tinsel into their ponytails, and were feeling fizzy with Christmas excitement.

"It's going to be fun to learn how to make crackers," said Rachel. "Mum said that she'd come and buy some for

Christmas Day."

All the crackers were going to be sold at the Tippington Community Centre Christmas Fair that afternoon.

"What will happen to the money we raise at the fair?" Kirsty asked.

"Fingers crossed there will be enough to give the community centre a new coat of paint," said Rachel. "It looks a bit tatty!"

They looked up at the building. It was faded and weather-beaten, and the old paint was starting to peel off. The only thing that made it jolly was the banner hanging above the door, held up with glittering threads of tinsel:

'ECO CRACKER WORKSHOP
TODAY'

Inside, the room was sparkling with

garlands of tinsel. Wooden tables were arranged in a big square and covered with long, red cloths. There were different craft materials on each table. The girls could see bowls filled with cardboard tubes, colourful paper hats, red ribbon and stripy red-and-white string.

Read Konnie the Christmas Cracker Fairy to find out what adventures are in store for Kirsty and Rachel!

Calling all parents, carers and teachers!
The Rainbow Magic fairies are here to help
your child enter the magical world of reading.
Whatever reading stage they are at, there's
a Rainbow Magic book for everyone!
Here is Lydia the Reading Fairy's guide to
supporting your child's journey at all levels.

Starting Out

Our Rainbow Magic Beginner Readers are perfect for first-time readers who are just beginning to develop reading skills and confidence. Approved by teachers, they contain a full range of educational levelling, as well as lively full-colour illustrations.

Developing Readers

Rainbow Magic Early Readers contain longer stories and wider vocabulary for building stamina and growing confidence. These are adaptations of our most popular Rainbow Magic stories, specially developed for younger readers in conjunction with an Early Years reading consultant, with full-colour illustrations.

Going Solo

The Rainbow Magic chapter books - a mixture of series and one-off specials - contain accessible writing to encourage your child to venture into reading independently. These highly collectible and much-loved magical stories inspire a love of reading to last a lifetime.

www.orchardseriesbooks.co.uk

"Rainbow Magic got my daughter reading chapter books. Great sparkly covers, cute fairies and traditional stories full of magic that she found impossible to put down" - Mother of Edie (6 years)

"Florence LOVES the Rainbow Magic books. She really enjoys reading now" - Mother of Florence (6 years)

Read along the Reading Rainbow!

Well done – you have completed the book!

This book was worth 4 stars.

See how far you have climbed on the Reading Rainbow.
The more books you read, the more stars you can colour in
and the closer you will be to becoming a Royal Fairy!

Do you want to print your own Reading Rainbow?

1) Go to the Rainbow Magic website

2) Download and print out the poster

3) Colour in a star for every book you finish
and climb the Reading Rainbow

4) For every step up the rainbow,
you can download your very own certificate

There's all this and lots more at
orchardseriesbooks.co.uk

You'll find activities, stories, a special newsletter
AND you can search for the fairy with your name!